Invisible Me

Also by Debbi Mack

Identity Crisis

Least Wanted

Riptide

Deep Six

Five Uneasy Pieces

Invisible Me

Debbi Mack

Best wishes,
Debbi Mack

Renegade Press

Savage, MD

Renegade Press
P.O. Box 156
Savage, MD

This is a work of fiction. Any resemblance to actual events
or persons, living or dead, is entirely coincidental.

Library of Congress Cataloging-in-Publication Data
Invisible Me by Debbi Mack
ISBN: 978-0-9829508-8-3
Library of Congress Control Number: 2014948320

For Rick

CHAPTER 1

My name is Portia Maddox. Last week, I turned thirteen. Hands on her hips, my grandma looked me in the eye and said, "My, you're turning into a little lady." Yeah, right.

Technically, I'm a teenager, but I feel no different than when I was twelve. My parents seem to think this birthday is a BFD. But I'm just the same old me.

There are a few things you should know. My father's in the military. That means we move a lot. I've gone to about a hundred different schools in the last six years. Maybe a few less. People tell me I exaggerate.

You may be thinking, "What kind of name is Portia, anyway?" Well, my parents chose it because they are Shakespeare freaks. Portia's a character from *The Merchant of Venice*. I haven't read the play yet, but I hear Portia is smart, beautiful, and rich. That means the only thing we have in common is the name. Who cares? As names go, it's so sixteenth century. Being stuck with it is a cross I must bear. And believe me, I have more than my share of those.

My life hasn't been easy. We've moved so many times, the moment I start to fit in and make friends, it's time to leave.

Oh, yeah. One other thing. I'm an albino. That's a pigment-free person. I'm talking white skin and hair, with pink eyes like a white rabbit or a gerbil. Nice, huh? You're probably thinking, she won't be entering any beauty contests any time soon.

Did you know that many think albinos are evil? It's not true, of course. I think the rumor gained traction in that stupid book by Dan Brown—*The Da Vinci Code*.

Have you read it? If not, I'll save you the trouble. It's about how the Catholic Church is weird and evil. Albinos are even more weird and evil than the church, and it's amazing what people can do in 24 hours if they don't eat or sleep. And, according to the book, the Louvre museum in Paris is a dangerous place. That's it. You're welcome.

I attend Jefferson Davis Junior High near Pensacola, Florida, where my dad is stationed. It's in the very deep South. Southerners have a take on the Civil War that's vastly different from what I learned in Newport, Rhode Island. As a matter of fact, Florida and Rhode Island might as well be on different planets.

Anyhow, it's a typical day at school. Everyone is stealing glances at me or going out of their way to not look at me. Today begins my fourth week at the New School of the Month. We've passed the stage where the kids mutter, "freak" or "Hi, Whitey" (followed by the inevitable snickers), or go dumb as posts, gawking or turning away in horror when they see me. I am now merely a curiosity. I figure my classmates either accept my appearance or have grown less disgusted by it. Whatever. I take their behavior with a grain of salt, the way I accept anything that's inevitable. Like the coldness of winter, or the notion that I'll die someday. Hey, we all have to deal with these and other harsh realities. I figure my lack of pigmentation has given me a head start.

I'm sitting alone in the cafeteria, poking at the mystery lunch meat, when someone brushes against me. I hear a light tap on the bench next to where I'm sitting. I glance over at a folded piece of paper.

Looking up, I see the back of Denise Laughton's blonde head retreating. The most popular girl in my class takes her place at a table with her many followers. It's the same drill every day. She glances my way. It happens so fast, I can't be sure. Maybe I imagined it.

I pick up the paper and open it. Inside, a message is written in purple ink. Beautiful penmanship. So different from my own sloppy scrawl.

The note reads: *Please meet me after school by the gym. It's a matter of life and death. Thanks, D.L.*

CHAPTER 2

After seventh period, I wander by the gym, half-wondering if I'm being set up or about to be the butt of another practical joke. Lingering by the door, ready to bolt, I hear "psst." I step into the gym and see Denise standing against a wall a few feet away.

She waves me over. "C'mon. Hurry." Her voice is pinched. She looks frantic.

"What? Afraid to be seen with the freakazoid chick?"

She grabs my arm and pulls me toward the bleachers. We duck underneath.

I cross my arms. "Well, I guess that answers my question."

"Hey, look, I'm sorry." Her voice catches. It's enough for me to stand down a bit. "I wanted to talk to you because I have a problem. And I can't discuss it with my friends."

I roll my eyes. "Are you serious? Take my advice. Don't go into sales."

As I turn to leave, she yanks me back. "I didn't mean it the way it sounded. Please, please listen to me."

She sounds desperate. I can scarcely believe the most popular girl in my class is begging me for help.

I sigh. "Fine. What is it?"

"It's my boyfriend, Randy. I think he might be seeing another girl."

She tells me about Kathleen, a girl she met over the summer in tennis camp. They became doubles partners. Denise introduced Kathleen to all her friends, Randy included. Kathleen goes to another school. I tune out and stifle a yawn. *This is a life-or-death problem?* "I need you to follow Randy," she says. "Find out if he's seeing her."

"What? Are you kidding? Why don't you follow him yourself?"

"Because he'll notice me. I need someone he doesn't know."

I laugh. "And I'm the one to do it? Look at me. I don't exactly blend with the scenery."

"I've got that figured. My sister's in a theater group. She'll borrow a wig. You can wear it with a hat and dark glasses. He'll never spot you."

I start to protest. Why did she choose me? I'm the new kid and I'm a freak. Ah, that's why she chose me. Which leaves me with one question.

"Why should I do this?"

Denise leans in and whispers, as if sharing a government top secret. "If you do, I'll invite you to my birthday party next month."

CHAPTER 3

For a moment, I'm too stunned to speak.

Denise Laughton's upcoming birthday bash is the talk of the school. Getting asked is like receiving an invite to Miley Cyrus's coming-out party.

Denise is talking but I'm not paying strict attention. She shoves a photo of a girl in my face. She's a pretty redhead with impish green eyes.

"You know Randy, of course," Denise says. I nod numbly. "If you see him with Kathleen" —she cocks her head toward the photo— "just let me know."

"Um, okay." Apparently, we've struck a deal. Or so Denise thinks.

I consider saying no, but Denise's offer entices me. I feel a sudden rush of power. *Ha! Look who needs who!*

φφφ

The next day after school, I see Randy and Denise talking. They say their goodbyes and he strides across the street, stopping long enough to give Denise a final wave before disappearing around a corner.

I'm on my bike, my colorless hair tucked under a ridiculous blonde wig. A baseball cap perches atop the monstrosity. Denise has provided light-colored foundation with sunscreen, which I've liberally applied to my pale cheeks and other exposed body parts. In case you haven't heard, albinos burn easily. My eyes are hidden behind dark glasses. I look like the world's lamest spy.

I set off on my bike, keeping a good distance between Randy and me.

If you bike, you know that maintaining a distance between yourself and a pedestrian is difficult. I keep stopping so I won't get too close to him. Meanwhile, God knows where Randy's headed. I figure it can't be all that far if he's traveling on foot.

Turns out I'm wrong. Randy makes a right onto a four-lane road. He halts at a sheltered bus stop. I circle back. By the time I've returned, an ECAT bus (that stands for Escambia County Area Transit—big time, huh?) is pulling up. Randy boards it. The doors close and the bus takes off. I follow in hot pursuit.

The bus is slow-moving and makes frequent stops. That makes it easy for me to keep up. Randy gets off near a busy intersection and waits, for what I don't know. I turn down the nearest side street and hide next to a tree where I can observe him unnoticed.

He is tall and slender with glossy brown hair. Cute, but not overly so. He has a way of shoving his hands deep into his pockets, as if he wants to hide them. I find that oddly cute. His nose is a bit crooked, as if it had been broken and not properly set. He looks very serious. He must have a lot on his mind. Is he worried because he's cheating on Denise?

Or is he worried about the crazy girl in the blonde wig who's been following him?

Another bus wheezes to the curb and Randy gets on. As the doors shut and the bus lumbers off, I cycle behind it. This works well until the bus signals to make a turn onto Route 29, a major highway and bike-unfriendly road. I may be pale, but I'm not suicidal. I coast past, turning my head to watch the bus roar onto the highway. Randy escapes, free and clear, despite my amazing surveillance skills.

CHAPTER 4

I've barely arrived at school the next day, when Denise runs up to me.

"So? What happened? Where did he go?"

"Down, girl," I say. "He got on a bus and transferred to another bus, which turned onto Route 29. From there, all I can tell you is he went south. Not having a death wish, I aborted the mission."

Denise looks crushed. "Where would he go that requires taking Route 29?"

"Good question."

"Now what?"

"Next time I could hop on the bus and see where he goes." It's the only thing I can suggest.

She beams. "Awesome. That's a great idea. I can't wait until next week."

"Mm-hmm. Want to get together and hang out or something?" These words tumble out. Oops. My cheeks turn hot. I brace myself to be rejected. I'm an expert at it.

Denise looks thoughtful. It seems to take a lot of effort.

She grins. "I'm heading to the mall with a couple of friends after school today. Want to come along?"

Oh, my God. She's going to let her friends see us together.

I nod and smile. Works for me.

I head for the caf at noon, wondering if Denise is ready to share a meal with me in public. A chubby, black girl appears at my elbow.

"Hi," she says, out of breath. "My name's Judy Lee."

"Hi, Judy." I recognize her from math class.

"Mind if I eat with you today?"

I stop so short, Judy nearly loses her balance. *Why am I suddenly so popular?*

"I'm sorry," Judy says, sounding timid. "You don't even know me. Never mind."

She starts to turn away. I stop her with a hand on her arm.

"No, I'm sorry. It's just . . . no one usually wants to be seen with me."

Judy looks wary. "Yeah, well . . ." Her voice trails off. She continues her labored breathing. "I don't have a lot of friends either."

"Are you all right?"

"What do you mean?"

"You sound out of breath."

Judy's smile contrasts sharply with her complexion. "Oh that. I have asthma. Sometimes it acts up. No biggie."

We stand momentarily like a pair of rocks in a stream, students flowing around us.

"Well, Judy. I'm starving."

"Me, too." Her coffee-colored eyes light up.

"Let's get something to eat."

φφφ

As we down our pizza and soda, Judy starts talking about her family. She has a younger brother and an older sister.

"It must be nice," I say. "I'm an only child. It's lonely. Especially when you're as . . . different as I am. And your family's always moving."

"My sis is in high school now," she says. "We're only two years apart. When we've gone to the same school, I've been able to hang out with her. She's pretty popular, but . . . well, not me. Haven't made too many friends in my own class."

"Why? What's the problem?"

"My sister has much lighter skin. Like my brother. They take after my mom. My dad is black as the ace of spades."

She laughs at her own joke. I don't know how to react. Should I laugh? That seems cruel.

"How ironic."

"What do you mean?"

"People shun you because you're too black and they shun me because I'm too white."

I crack a smile. She starts laughing so hard, she's gulping breaths and shedding tears. I start laughing along with her.

Before we split up after lunch, Judy asks if I'll help her with math.

"You're so good at it," she says. "Want to come over tonight? I live only a few blocks from here."

I pause and consider her question. I wonder how long I'll be at the mall with Denise.

"Could we make it tomorrow?"

Judy nods like a bobble-head doll. "Sure, thanks," she says, trying to catch her breath. "I'm really glad we had lunch today."

"Me, too." I feel an unfamiliar rush of warmth. Judy's smile gleams. "Well, I'll see you later. Lunch tomorrow?" I nod. She turns and moves toward her locker.

I stand for a moment, pondering life's odd turns. Here I am, the biggest nerd—hair and skin so white they look bleached. Yet, suddenly, kids are seeking my counsel. Part of me isn't surprised, because I can learn most subjects with ease. And there are few subjects I'm not interested in.

One summer, I tried reading an old encyclopedia at the library. The volumes weighed a ton each. I started with A and plowed through most of it. I call tell you plenty about aardvarks, apples, agnostics, atriums, and aviaries. Not to mention albinism.

You know the expression "encyclopedic knowledge"? The term is misleading. If I learned one thing from reading them, it's that encyclopedias don't cover everything.

CHAPTER 5

After school, I'm standing out front, waiting for Denise. I check my watch. She's running about five minutes late. I'm wondering if she's full of shit about going shopping, when she approaches with two other girls.

"Hey, Portia," she says. Her smile is unforced, her voice lilting. "Portia, these are my friends, Mindy and Tara."

"Hi." I can't help but notice the way the two girls are staring at me. They look frightened.

"It's okay," I joke. "You won't catch what I have. I suffer from lack of pigmentation, not leprosy."

Denise laughs. "You're really funny, you know that?" She laughs again. Mindy and Tara chuckle.

"Well, if I couldn't laugh . . ." I leave the thought unfinished.

"I know what you mean." For a moment, Denise looks sad. I wonder if she's thinking about Randy and what he might be up to behind her back.

Denise perks up. "My mom will be here anytime now. She'll give us a ride to the mall."

I nod. I've already told my mom I'll be going to the mall with some girls instead of coming right home. I texted her while waiting for Denise and her friends. She texted back, "Good. Have a great time."

I realize she hasn't asked what time I'll be home, who the kids are, or where I'm having dinner. I wonder if she's so floored that I'm hanging out at the mall with anyone that she forgot to ask.

φφφ

Denise's mother picks us up in a glossy black Beemer. Like Denise, her hair is blonde. Unlike her daughter, it's styled. And she's all duded up in a blue suit and pearls, as if she just stepped from a corporate boardroom. My mother goes around in jeans or sweats.

Hmm, I think. Not your typical soccer mom.

A chorus of "Hi, Mrs. Laughton!" erupts from Mindy and Tara, as we scramble into the car.

"Hi, Mindy. Tara." Mrs. Laughton cranes her neck and bestows a pearly white smile. "Hi, sweetie." She leans toward Denise, poised to give her daughter a peck on the cheek. Denise recoils. "You haven't introduced me to your new friend," Mrs. Laughton says. She sounds happy. *Too happy. How can anyone be that cheerful?*

Denise introduces us. "Um, Mom, this is Portia. Portia, this is my mom."

"What a beautiful name," says Mrs. Laughton, sounding rather dreamy. She catches my grimace in the rear-view mirror. "Your name is charming," she assures me.

Yeah. Right.

φφφ

Mrs. Laughton pulls up to the mall and delivers a final set of instructions about what time she'll pick us up and where. She calls it the "pick-up point." Well, duh! "Please don't be late, okay?" Big pearly white smile. "Have a great time, girls."

We explode from the car and race toward the entrance. I'm giggling and rushing through the automatic sliding door. Mindy and Tara bounce a few steps behind Denise, whose blonde hair reminds me of a flapping golden flag. I let them lead the way down the main hall with its shiny marble-tiled floors. The air conditioning feels cool against my skin. I smell cookies or pretzels. The girls slow down as we approach the central court, where several people are milling about—a good-sized crowd of mall rats from my age to late teens and a few mothers pushing baby carriages or guiding toddlers by the hand. Denise reaches the railing, leaning against it as if staking a claim. Tara and Mindy hover, ladies in waiting to the princess.

"So, where do you guys want to go?" Denise asks.

"Old Navy," Tara says.

"That's old news! Hot Topic!" Mindy pipes up.

"Old Navy!"

"Hot Topic!"

I glance around. Wow, this place is overwhelming. Slightly dizzying even. The ceiling has lots of skylights and reaches halfway to the stars. Sunbeams wash over everything, making the place gleam. Plastic palm trees and flowers are arranged in the fake stone planters. I spot a bookstore across the way. It's all I can do to restrain myself from running over there.

"Well, let's ask Portia," Denise says, snapping me from my reverie.

"Huh?"

"Old Navy or Hot Topic?"

As a card-carrying nerd, I have no opinion and I couldn't care less. But it seems best to play along. Which store should I choose?

CHAPTER 6

After a moment's pause, I say, "We have plenty of time. Why don't we go to both?"

Denise smiles. "You're so smart." Tara and Mindy look befuddled. After a bit more discussion we settle on Hot Topic. Mindy seems to be more assertive than Tara. We wander over to the store, where, following Denise's lead, the girls find things for me to try on.

"Oh, look! This is perfect for you." Denise hustles toward me, with a pair of hip hugger jeans and cute cropped top with a sparkly heart decal.

"Honestly, you shouldn't," I say. "I didn't bring any money."

Mindy and Tara float about, holding items up and posing before the large mirrors. Despite my protests, they keep recommending clothes for me to try on. They don't seem to understand that I have no money.

Sitting on a chair tucked in among the racks, I make myself as small as possible. Can I will myself into invisibility? What an interesting idea for a short story. Maybe I'll write it someday.

That would be the most awesome job, wouldn't it? To be a writer. To write stories about kids who could do things like think themselves into invisibility. Because when you're a writer, you can make almost anything happen.

Denise walks up. "We're going to Old Navy. Are you sure you don't want anything here?" She holds up a pair of faded cutoff jeans with frayed bottoms like Daisy Duke would wear.

φφφ

After a quick tour of Old Navy—nothing of interest—we make our way around the perimeter of the mall, stopping here and there. Because we eat dinner early at our house, I feel hungry and pick up a soft pretzel in the food court. Amazing! I text my mom and ask her to set aside my dinner. I keep thinking about the bookstore but don't mention it.

Tara checks her watch. "Hey, Denise. Isn't your mom coming soon?"

Denise, looking at a group of guys, snaps to attention. "Oh, right. Everyone have everything?"

Tara holds up her shopping bags. "You bet."

Mindy holds up her bags. "Sure thing."

I hold up my one bag with the new pair of jorts Denise bought for me. "Yeah."

CHAPTER 7

When I get home my mother looks distracted. She asks about my day and what I did at the mall, but I can tell her mind is elsewhere. I put on my new purchase and model for her. She nods and smiles, but she's got this odd look as if she were seeing right through me.

Fine, whatever, I say to myself. Be that way. They're just a pair of jorts. It's not like I cured cancer or something.

I do my homework and then eat the dinner my mother has kept warm in the oven: baked chicken breast and mashed potatoes with gravy. She takes a salad from the refrigerator. I eat while watching Doctor Who on TV.

"Where's Dad?" I ask, between mouthfuls of mashed potatoes.

"He's working late, honey."

"He's doing that a lot these days."

"I know."

She sounds sad. Or maybe it's my imagination.

People tell me, "Portia, you think too much." Well, I also think I feel too much. You know?

φφφ

The next day is Friday. Thank God. I make my way through the crowded hall. The kids are jostling me. I'm getting the hairy eyeball from the usual suspects. I've learned to ignore them. This time I get up the nerve to stare back at one. He turns away. Ha!

When the last bell rings, I go to my locker and open it. I'm looking forward to two whole days away from these people. I'm shuffling books, when someone taps my shoulder.

I jump.

"Hi, Portia."

It's Judy. I relax and let out my breath.

"Hi, Judy."

"Are you okay?"

"I'm fine. I'm just in a hurry to get out of here."

Judy nods. "I know how you feel." She seems anxious. Then I remember the asthma. Her breathing problems. That must suck.

"I was wondering about, you know, getting together . . ." Judy says. She sounds almost afraid to say the words.

I remember our date. "To study math? Sure. What time works for you?"

"You want to walk home with me after school?"

I nod. "Sure."

φφφ

I manage to make it through the following week intact. For some reason, I haven't caught sight of Denise all day. When I looked around at lunch, I noticed Tara and Mindy sharing a table. I raised my hand briefly to say hi, but they either didn't see me or they ignored me. Figures.

Judy walks up. I finish texting my mom that I won't be coming home after school. For the second time in two days, I'll be hanging out at a friend's house.

"Hey, what's your home number?" I ask. "My mom likes to know this stuff. Just in case my cell phone dies or something." I say this as if I'm always going over to other kids' houses. What a laugh.

Judy hesitates. "I ... don't have one."

"What?"

She bows her head. "Our phone was disconnected last week."

She mumbles the words, but I hear her plain as day.

I reach out and touch her arm.

"Don't worry. I won't tell anyone."

CHAPTER 8

To get to Judy's house, we walk three blocks west and four
blocks south of school to a dead end. We keep walking.
After tromping through the woods, we emerge onto what
amounts to a wide dirt lane. Judy points to a house and says,
"That's my place."

We cross over the dirt lane. The sun-baked earth is
packed down hard as concrete.

Judy lives in what I've heard people call a "cracker
house." Not fancy, but not a shack, either. Old, but tidy. The
green shutters stand out against the whitewashed wooden
exterior. A columned porch extends across the front, the tin
roof sloping down to shelter a porch swing, a glider, and a
wicker rocker. Some people might think it's corny, but to me,
it looks like a cozy place.

I take a deep breath. "What's that awesome smell?" I ask.

"Heliotrope," Judy says. "It grows all over."

Lucky you, I think.

"And we've got roses." Judy points to a bush covered in
gorgeous blooms.

She lumbers up the creaky front steps. I follow her. She pauses to fish the key out of her purse and unlock the door.

"My ma won't be home for half an hour," she explains.

I nod. I wonder what her ma does, but I don't ask. I figure if she wants to tell me, she will. My mom stays home. She says we don't stay in one place long enough for her to take a real job. I've often wondered about this. It doesn't seem fair. Unless my mom really wants to stay home and let dad take care of everything. But that isn't like her at all. My mom is the kind of person who's always telling me I can be anything I want to be. So how did she end up being what she is?

I'm thinking all these stupid thoughts as we walk into Judy's house. We enter a small, cozy living room. All the furniture is old and worn. Mismatched. It hits me. I've never known anyone who's poor.

I keep walking, trying to look unfazed, but I have zero social skills. Am I blushing or is there a strange look on my face? I wonder. Judy, to her credit, doesn't seem to notice a thing.

One piece of furniture looks really comfy. An old sofa with royal-blue plush cushions. I love plush cushions. They're so soft. I run my hand across the top of the sofa. It's as smooth and soft as I imagine it. I catch a glimpse of a yellow cat. I'm so preoccupied, I step on its tail. It lets out a screech and races from me. Way to make a good impression. I give Judy an apologetic look. "I'm sorry. I didn't realize it was so close."

Judy snorts and waves a hand. "That cat. She's always underfoot. Hey, you want some lemonade? Or ice tea? Both made fresh."

I go for the lemonade.

While Judy's getting our drinks, I try to find her cat and convince her I'm not there to kill her.

"What's your cat's name?" I ask.

"Marmalade."

"Here Marmalade," I call, repeatedly, ducking down to check under furniture. No kitty. Oh, well.

Judy comes out with large glasses, filled nearly to the rim with light yellow fluid, bits of pulp swirling about among the ice cubes. Condensation runs down the sides of the glasses.

"So ... let's go to my room and get started."

"Right." Omigosh. I nearly forgot. I'm here to help Judy with her math. Jeez, I'm such an idiot sometimes.

φφφ

An hour later, Judy and I are both feeling pretty mathed out. During that time, Judy's mom came home and poked her head in long enough to say hello and meet me. We've gone over quadratic equations and other fun stuff we've learned in seventh grade that will only get tougher as time goes by and the grade level gets higher. Judy is still struggling with one particular equation, but she's game to figure it out. And that counts for a lot, in my book.

"Why don't we take a break?" I suggest. "Sometimes it helps to step away from a problem. If you think about other things, then come back to it, you often find that the solution will come to you."

Judy scowls. "Well . . ." She's determined. I like that.

"Just ten minutes helps," I say.

She smiles in that way that lights up the room. "Oh, what the heck. I've been trying for years to understand math. What's ten minutes?"

"Look," I say. "Why don't we do something else for a while? Anything at all."

"Girls!" It's Judy's mom. She raps on the door and opens it. Mrs. Lee has a much lighter complexion than her daughter, but her eyes look just like Judy's. "I'm going to start dinner. Portia, would you like to stay and eat with us?"

Judy turns to me. "Yes, Portia, would you like to stay for dinner?" Her eyes plead for me to agree.

I nod and say, "Yeah, I'd like that very much. Thank you. I'd better text my mom and let her know."

For a moment, Judy's mom just stares at my cell phone. "Those are very handy, aren't they?"

I nod.

"I must get one soon," she says. She sounds like she's talking to herself. As she shuts the door, I hear her say, "All the kids have them . . . ."

Silence roars in my ears.

"Hey!" Judy says, "I'll get some more lemonade. And we can play a videogame. How about that?"

I manage a smile. "Sounds good."

Judy goes off to get our lemonade.

I could just die.

CHAPTER 9

I manage to text my mom before Judy comes back with our drinks. Which is nice, because I feel like an idiot. I don't need to make matters worse by sending texts in front of her, you know?

While I'm thinking this, I'm also thinking that I'm even more idiotic and full of myself than I originally thought. Judy walks in with the drinks and says, "You want to play Happy Hamster? It's kind of like Sonic the Hedgehog, but different. It's an old game, but I love it."

"Okay, I guess. I'm not usually very good at computer games. And I've never played Sonic. How does it work?"

"Well, in my game, you try to raise this hamster to higher and higher levels. All these obstacles appear. And you have a limited amount of time to move the hamster past them. It's a little tricky, at first. But it's fun."

"Okay." It seems only fair for me to try it. I'm good at math and I came there to help Judy out. Maybe, in return, Judy can help me with something I'm not good at.

Mrs. Lee calls to us that it'll be fifteen minutes until dinner. I'm so focused on playing Happy Hamster, this news barely registers. I'm having repeated problems getting my hamster, named Jake, past the water hazard. Jake has drowned so many times, I've lost count. That horrible gurgling sound will haunt my nightmares.

It's not that I'm such a competitive person. It's just that the thought of little Jake dying again has become unbearable. I have to remind myself it's all a game.

I must look really crushed, because Judy lays a hand on my shoulder and says, "Don't worry. The more you do this, the better you get at it."

When Mrs. Lee calls us to dinner, I reluctantly turn the remote control over to Judy, who hits the button. The screen goes all blue. Game over.

"I hope you like cornbread," Judy says. "My mom makes the best cornbread ever. From scratch."

I nod. My mom makes it, but from packaged mix. Where does a working mom find the time to do that? Maybe it doesn't take much time. Well, there I go again. Thinking. Too much thinking.

I follow Judy into the dining area, which is actually a small table set against the wall right near the kitchen. A TV set is on the table, placed against the wall, like a jukebox in a diner. The table is set for five, with almost no room for elbows.

"Okay, Judy," Mrs. Lee says, grabbing a plate from the table and spooning green vegetables onto it from a pan. "Sarah can sit next to you, with Portia on the other side. Louis can sit next to Sarah. I'll sit next to Louis at the end, so I can get up if I need to."

She runs over and places the plate on the table, then shakes her head. "I must be losing my mind." She backtracks to the oven and grabs the pan, then circles the table, spooning the vegetables onto the plates. "Sarah! Louis!

Dinner! Judy, could you please tell your sister and brother dinner is served?"

"Can I help you?" I ask Mrs. Lee.

"No, no. You're our guest." She pulls out a chair. "Please have a seat. We'll take care of everything."

I take my place. She's allowed me the most space. The others are squeezed together like sardines. Mrs. Lee's spot is so tight, there is no room for a placemat.

I wonder where Mr. Lee is. *Don't ask. Just keep your mouth shut.*

A boy with a complexion to match Judy's, maybe seven years old, skips into the room. "I'm so hungry," he moans. I assume this is Louis. This thought is confirmed when Mrs. Lee introduces him as Judy's younger brother.

Judy and another girl, taller and with lighter skin, come in. "Sarah, this is my friend, Portia. And this is my sister, Sarah."

"Hi, Sarah," I say. "Judy has told me about you."

Sarah is chunky like Judy but not, as Judy has put it, "black as the ace of spades." Which reminds me again of Mr. Lee. I keep wondering where he is. Should I ask Judy later? Wait until next week at school? I scold myself. Why do I keep thinking about this? It's none of my business. What in the world is wrong with me? Why am I always thinking about stuff like this?

"I hope you like chicken."

"I do," I say, as Mrs. Lee comes over with a large platter of pan-fried chicken. It smells like heaven. You could bottle the aroma as perfume. After Louis slides in next to his mother, Mrs. Lee introduces us all again.

Mrs. Lee makes polite conversation. Although I am not good at small talk, I keep up as best I can.

"What do your parents do, Portia?" Mrs. Lee asks.

"My dad's in the military. My mom just stays home."

"Your mom doesn't just stay home, you know," she says. "There's plenty of work to do around the house. Some people don't have a clue about how much work stay-at-home moms do."

Then, how do you manage to do what you do? I want to ask her. How do you find time to make cornbread from scratch? And where the heck is Mr. Lee?

"I was just telling my husband last night that, since he works night shifts and sleeps during the day, he has no idea what goes on here." Mrs. Lee chuckles and shakes her head.

Yeah, I think. And neither do I.

"Portia's lucky," Judy says. She turns to me. "You've lived all over the country, haven't you?"

"Yes, I've lived all over." I fake a laugh. "Lucky me."

Everyone keeps eating, except Mrs. Lee. Her forehead furrows and she peers at me.

"Where are you from originally?" she asks.

"I'm not from anywhere in particular," I say. "I'm from all over. My home is wherever I happen to be at the time. The *entire* world is my home, okay?"

The words pour out, as if Mrs. Lee has pushed a red button and opened a floodgate.

In a soft voice, she asks, "How long have you lived here in town, Portia?"

"Four. Whole. Weeks. Almost." I spew the four simple words. A long silence follows them. Everyone looks at me.

When will I ever learn to keep my mouth shut?

CHAPTER 10

During dessert—homemade apple pie—Judy invites me to
see a movie the next night. Frankly, I'm amazed she's still
speaking to me after I acted like such an idiot. But I tell her
I'd like to go.

"Thanks for inviting me over, Judy," I say, as I prepare to
leave. At least I've remembered a basic rule of etiquette.

"How are you getting home?" Judy asks.

"I'll call my Mom. She'll pick me up."

"Are you sure? My Mom could give you a ride."

I briefly consider asking Mrs. Lee for a ride home, but I
acted so rude at dinner. I'm embarrassed to ask.

"My mom will come. What's your address?"

"We don't have one," Judy says. "Our mail goes to a post
office box." I put my hand up. "Got it covered. I'll pick an
easy spot for her to find." I figure I'll cross the dirt road,
backtrack through the woods and meet her at the nearest
corner.

I thank Mrs. Lee for her hospitality. She stops doing the
dishes and wipes her hands on a towel.

"Portia," she says, bending over and placing a hand on my arm. "It was very nice to meet you. Are you sure I can't give you a ride home?"

"That's okay." I'd do anything to avoid the uncomfortable silence between us during the long ride.

She nods, as if she understands. "I really am glad you stayed for dinner. Judy doesn't bring a lot of friends over. So, feel free to come by anytime, okay?"

φφφ

I leave Judy's house and cross the dirt path. Through the woods I go to the dead-end street. I call my mom. We arrange to meet at the nearest intersection. I figure I'll pick a house and tell her that's where Judy lives. No harm, no foul, right?

Ten minutes later, Mom pulls up in her Subaru wagon. I get in.

"Which one is your friend's house?" I point to the blue house on the corner. 5151 Dixie Hill Circle is painted on the mailbox. I stow the information for future reference. How hard is that?

My Mom peers at the house. "Hmm. Why are all the lights out?"

One glance tells me she's right. I hadn't even noticed. The gig is up.

I recover. "Everyone went to the store," I lie. "I think they had to pick up something from the pharmacy."

"Mom shrugs and pulls away from the curb.

I breathe a sigh of relief, but I think, *That's it? No more questions?*

"By the way," she says, negotiating a left turn onto the main road, "a girl called the house looking for you. She sounded frantic."

"Who?" I can't begin to imagine.

"Denise, I think."

Oh, my God! I never gave Denise my cell phone number. She must be desperate to have tracked me down at home.

"Don't you remember Denise?" I say. "Yesterday I went to the mall with her and a couple of her friends."

Mom slaps her forehead. "Oh, of course. I thought that name sounded familiar." Her nervous laugh sounds fake.

Yeah, right.

We ride home in silence.

CHAPTER 11

Once home, I head straight to my room. I want privacy. No need for my mother to hear my conversations with Denise. In fact, my life isn't her concern. She doesn't seem to care all that much, anyway. I may not be the greatest student or most amazing person in the entire universe, but you'd think she'd be interested that her daughter—someone who possibly qualifies as the single most socially backward kid on the planet—has made a few friends since arriving in this dinky little town.

I start to punch Denise's number into my cell, but I don't know it. Duh! What a doofus I am.

I head downstairs where my parents are watching TV. For a change, my dad is home. We are almost like a normal family—whatever that means.

As I approach the living room, I hear my parents whispering. I creep toward the living room, staying out of sight while straining to hear their conversation over the chatter from the television.

"I know it's been tough lately," my dad says.

"We need to talk about it," my mom says.

"Especially with Portia getting to that age. She's smart. She's going to start asking questions."

Hearing my name paralyzes me.

Questions about what? What on earth are they talking about?

A commercial blares. Someone hits the mute and the house goes silent.

"I guess we can cross that bridge when we get to it." I hear my dad's voice getting louder. So, I act like I'm just coming down the hall.

As I approach, my dad appears. "Portia, darling!" he says.

With a hand under each armpit, my dad lifts me up. When I was a little girl, he used to do this all the time. It was cute then. It's not so cute now. But I still love that he does it. And I don't know how to tell him to stop. Or if I should.

CHAPTER 12

My father smiles broadly. My mother is on the sofa, staring into space. The TV show is back, with no sound. And I'm just hanging around.

"How ya' doing, Sweetie?"

"Great. Can you put me down now?"

My Dad laughs and twirls me around so my legs fly out, then he lowers me gently to the floor. My face is red. *I'm not in kindergarten,* I want to shout. I bite my tongue instead. Something about his treating me like a child appeals to me. Kinda. And it makes me feel very uncomfortable.

We are like strangers at a party. We have a connection but we don't have anything to say to each other.

He tousles my hair. This is what passes for conversation. "Mom, did you get Denise's number?"

She's staring at the silent TV. The sound of my voice brings her back. She snaps out of it and reaches for the phone. She enters the number and hands me the phone, then returns to zombie mode.

"Mom, are you okay?"

She blinks a few times. *Is she going to cry?* "I'm fine, honey."

She looks away. I swear to God, it looks like she's going to cry.

φφφ

I go to my room, feeling awful. What the hell is going on with my parents? Why is my Mom maybe crying? What does my Dad need to tell me? Why can't anything go right in my life, ever?

I dial Denise. Now my number will be on her caller ID. She answers on the second ring, sounding at her wit's end.

"Portia? Is that you?"

"Yeah. Hi, it's me."

"I need your help. Tomorrow. Okay?"

"What's going on?"

"It's Randy. I think he's going to meet Kathleen. I need you to follow him again."

I start to protest. I'm supposed to see a movie with Judy. I think about the birthday party. How can I juggle and do this? Maybe Judy won't mind if we reschedule. Maybe I can do both.

"Portia? Are you there?"

"I'm here. I hadn't planned on this."

"Oh, Portia," Denise whines. "I'll owe you big time, if you do me this favor. Please."

Excuse me. The most popular girl in school is begging *me* for a favor? And will owe *me* big time if I give it to her?

Who am I to deny her, right?

CHAPTER 13

Judy and I plan to catch the 4:00 show at the multiplex theater. Randy is supposed to catch the bus, maybe to see Kathleen, sometime around 3:30. Squeezing in both engagements will be physically impossible, especially for a thirteen-year-old kid with only a bicycle for transportation. I'm not getting my mother mixed up in this. She's got her own problems. Apparently.

The next afternoon I peddle to Judy's house. I sure wish she had a phone and I could have called her. Knocking on the door, I pray Mrs. Lee won't answer. I already feel lousy enough about breaking the date with Judy. The door creaks open and Judy's face appears. She's in weathered jeans and an old T-shirt.

"Portia! What's up?"

I try to look bummed out. It isn't hard.

φφφ

Judy takes the news really well. She says it would be fine if we got together tomorrow. Feeling relieved that Judy didn't give me a hard time, but bad about lying, I hop on my bike and head to Denise's place. Her house is halfway across town. Even though it's a small town, I pedal hard. By the time I reach Denise's, I'm panting. I've made up my mind. I'm going to catch that bus and follow Randy if it's the last thing I ever do.

When I pull up to the curb, Denise is standing there, arms crossed, prim as you please.

"Hi, Portia."

"Ugh," is all I can manage. "I assume you have a new spy outfit for me."

"Right. C'mon in." She strolls toward a columned mansion set behind a large green lawn that seems to go on forever.

I roll my bike into the driveway and park it near a hedge. I pick up my pace to join Denise. Up close, the house looks like a palace. Okay, I'm exaggerating a bit. But only a little.

Denise opens the door. We enter a foyer with marble floors and a great big chandelier made of diamonds. Or things that look like diamonds. Sparkly and colorful. Light twinkles off each piece.

I crane my head to gawk at this amazing fixture. It's gorgeous. Like the royal jewels arranged as a lighting source.

"Portia."

I ignore the faraway sound of my name and focus further on the chandelier.

"Portia."

My attention remains riveted on the fixture.

"Hey, Portia."

Pressure on my shoulder. It's Denise's hand.

"Portia," she says. "What's up? You need to catch the bus."

I right my head. Rubbing the base of my skull, I say, "Okay. Where's my disguise?"

Upstairs, in Denise's bedroom—a room so pink, it makes my eyes hurt—I get my new spy outfit, a red wig, baseball cap, and dark glasses. I put everything on and look at myself in the mirror. Today I am a ginger spy instead of a blonde bimbo. Awesome.

"Give me a minute," Denise calls from inside a closet the size of a backyard shed. "I've got the perfect top for you, if you're interested."

I yawn. *What are the chances we wear the same size?* I look around at the artwork on the walls. It's not what I'd expect in a thirteen-year-old's bedroom. One of them, a landscape in stark, bold colors, should hang in a gallery. Denise sashays out of her walk-in closet with something in her hand. She looks me over. "This color suits you."

"Thanks, I think."

Denise's brow wrinkles. "Portia, is something wrong?"

"No." I avoid her gaze.

We fall silent.

"Hey," I say. "Where's your family?" I'm just curious.

She shrugs. "I don't know."

In a lame attempt to smooth things over, I say, "Your mom seems really nice . . . ."

"Can we not talk about my mom?" Denise's voice is cold and hard as steel. She raises a hand to her mouth. She reddens. "Sorry."

"N-no problem," I stammer.

I remember the moment in the car when Mrs. Laughton leaned in to kiss Denise and how she recoiled.

Clearly, there's more going on here than meets the eye. And I haven't a clue.

CHAPTER 14

I'm breathless from pumping my bike pedals and thinking about how strange life can be. As if being an albino kid bouncing around the country like a pinball from place to place and school to school weren't challenging enough, things have become even more absurd. The prettiest and most popular girl in school has asked me to spy on her boyfriend who may be cheating on her, and she may have a big secret problem with her mother. Because I'm curious, I keep wondering what kind of problem? Serious? Abusive father? Physical violence? I can make myself crazy, thinking so much.

On top of this, I've lied to Judy, who deserves better. Why do I feel so guilty about this stuff? I hate that, too.

And my own parents are acting weird. Why is my mother so sad? What does my dad need to tell me? What's going on with them? I feel like I'm living in a soap opera.

I arrive at the stop where Randy caught the connecting bus the other day. I secure my bike to a nearby lamp post and await his arrival. I adjust my itchy wig. Checking the time on my cell, I know this is about the time Randy caught the bus a few days ago. But it's Saturday, and the schedule may be different. My stomach is doing flip-flops.

The bus pulls up and a few people emerge, including Randy. My heart skips a beat. My palms are sweaty. This is a new sensation. Why am I so nervous? What's wrong with me?

Am I nervous about following Randy? He's not even looking my way. Like before, he is waiting for the connecting bus, hands jammed into his pockets. He paces. I wonder what's on his mind. Is it Kathleen? Is it Denise? Have I blown my cover?

While I'm pondering these mysteries, a bus marked "Express" pulls up and Randy hops aboard. I follow, pay the fare and make my way down the aisle to the rear where I can keep an eye on him. I'm not losing him this time. No way.

CHAPTER 15

We roll down Route 29 toward the downtown area. After a while, the bus turns off the highway into a rundown industrial area of warehouses and old buildings. This doesn't square at all with the picture Denise has drawn about Randy and Kathleen. Maybe Randy looked anxious because he's mixed up with a girl from a bad neighborhood. I check to make sure Randy is still on the bus. He's there, all right, staring out the window.

I ease a finger between the wig and my head to scratch my itchy scalp. It's driving me nuts. I readjust the wig. I hope it looks normal. Or seminormal. Using my hand to wipe my damp brow, some of Denise's makeup comes off on my fingers. Great. I wipe them against the seatback. For the umpteenth time, I ask myself, *why don't I carry tissues?* I answer my own question. *Because I don't usually wear makeup! And I don't have allergies or cry a lot.* I don't need to carry a bunch of tissues, like some snot-nosed kid.

I glimpse an arm reaching up for the yellow cord. It's Randy's arm. He pulls the cord, slides off the seat and makes his way toward the front of the bus. Keeping my distance, I exit from the back door.

The bus lurches to a halt beside a gray cinderblock building. Randy, two old guys who look like they could use a hot bath, and I get off the bus. The old guys wander off. I follow Randy.

About five minutes later, we arrive at an old red-brick house in a shabby neighborhood. The yard is enclosed with a chain-link fence. Is this where Kathleen lives? If so, Randy is definitely slumming. Randy goes in.

When I cross the street to survey the building, my eyes land on a sign: "Escambia County Substance Abuse Facility."

Holy . . . . Denise is mistaken. Randy is up to something, and it's not Kathleen. I guess that's good news.

CHAPTER 16

The bad news is I have no idea why he is here or why he hasn't told Denise that he comes here. What's up with that? What am I going to tell Denise?

"Hey, Denise! Guess what? Randy's not cheating on you! But he may have a drug problem. Why don't you ask him? Ask him where he's been going every Tuesday."

I beat myself up over getting involved in this stupid plot.

All I wanted was to be liked. Is that bad? Stupid. Stupid.

Now, I have to figure out how to break the news to Denise that Randy isn't cheating, but is . . . what? A drug addict? Who knows?

I know one thing. I'm ready for some air-conditioning. Hanging out in the heat in an itchy wig and heavy makeup isn't my idea of fun.

I make my way up the walk to the rehab facility.

Inside, a pretty receptionist sits at a desk, a ledger open before her. She's on the phone. *Act young and helpless.* I wave my hand to catch her attention. "Excuse me," I murmur. "Could I use your restroom?"

She nods and jerks a thumb over her shoulder then covers the mouthpiece. "First door on the right," she says before returning to her call.

"Thanks." As good an excuse as any for regrouping and deciding my next move.

I've learned the hard way: Never pass up the opportunity to use a bathroom. I wash my hands, check my makeup, and blot my sweaty forehead with a paper towel. I look at myself in the mirror. What am I doing here? I don't recognize myself in this crazy outfit. Why did I let Denise dupe me into this?

After a final glance in the mirror to straighten my wig, I make tracks to find Randy.

I stroll down a long hall, its grayish-green walls sickly under fluorescent lights. A couple of guys in white coats shuffle by me. I pass a bunch of offices and rooms with single beds. But no sign of Randy. The occasional adult and teenager amble by. I try to keep a low profile. But how do you do that when you're an albino in dark glasses and a clownish red wig?

CHAPTER 17

I feel a tap on my shoulder and flinch.

"Excuse me." A man's voice. I'm having trouble hearing him. "Um, little girl?" *Who's he calling "little girl"? I'm a young lady. Where are his manners?*

Another shoulder tap. He is starting to piss me off.

"Excuse me, little girl."

Okay, that's it. I pivot, remove my sunglasses and confront him with my angriest pink-eyed glare. "What?"

He's in a brown suit. His eyebrows arch. His mouth opens slightly, then closes. I've shocked him. I know because I've seen this look before. Countless times.

He clears his throat. "Are you okay?"

"I'm fine, thank you." I let my gaze linger then replace my sunglasses. Like I need them indoors, anyway. I'm an albino, for God's sake, not a blind person, right?

"I'm Mr. Robinson. I work here," he says. "I couldn't help noticing you. You seem like you might be lost."

"Mr. Robinson, I'm fine." I smile, baring my teeth. "The thing is, I came in to use your restroom and, well, I guess I took a wrong turn. Anyway, I figured it couldn't be far and I wasn't going to take long, so . . . Have I broken any rules?"

I'm babbling and batting my eyeslashes. And I'm wearing sunglasses. Real genius.

"Visitors are supposed to sign in. We're pretty strict about these things."

To stave off a lecture, I break in. "I'm really, really sorry. I didn't know. If you want me to, I'll sign your book. I just needed a bathroom. All these hallways look alike, and I couldn't find it."

"That's okay, young lady." Mr. Robinson smiles and pats my shoulder. "Don't worry. You're not in trouble. Let's just not make a habit of this. Okay?"

I nod and breathe a sigh of relief. *I almost broke down and blubbered like a baby. Dodged that bullet.*

Mr. Robinson escorts me to the restroom then leaves. I wait a couple of minutes and resume my search. Near the end of the hall Randy rounds the corner and passes me, going the other way. I do a quick U-turn and follow at a safe distance.

He reaches the front desk and chats with the receptionist. They seem to be having a great time. Jeez! Is Randy cheating on Denise with her? She's old enough to be his mother! He signs out and leaves. I follow Randy through the seedy neighborhood to the bus stop and hang around far enough from view, so when the bus comes and he gets on, I run up behind him and jump on, too. Good God! I'm panting as I collapse onto the seat. Who knew being a spy could be so exhausting?

CHAPTER 18

Today, I'm going to the movies with Judy no matter what. My mom will drop me off at the house with no lights. I'm looking forward to this because I like her and I like the idea of doing something fun and normal for a change.

As I'm getting ready, Mom knocks on my door and sticks her head in. "Have you called your friend to let her know we're coming?"

"I can't. Their phone got ... it's not working right now."

She frowns. "Really?"

I shrug. "Some problem with their connection."

φφφ

I'm in the bathroom, slathering sunscreen on my face when my cell phone rings. It can wait. It's probably Denise. And I still haven't decided what to tell her about Randy.

Should I tell her the truth, or is that none of her business? Am I invading Randy's privacy?

Would it really hurt to tell Denise a little *white* lie? Oh, the irony!

I finish up, go to my bedroom, and retrieve my message from Denise. She sounds like she's going die of curiosity, if I don't call immediately. *Jeez! Get a grip*, I want to say to Denise. He's just a boy. He's cute, but enough is enough, okay?

I save Denise's rambling message and order my thoughts. I want to come up with a reply that makes sense.

When my mom drops me at Judy's "pretend" house, I'm relieved that she's on her way to meet a friend for coffee and doesn't ask to come in and meet Judy. I wave as she pulls away. *Thanks, Mom.*

φφφ

Judy's dad drops us off. I'm glad we're seeing a comedy. After buying buttered popcorn and Milk Duds, we find seats as the coming attractions roll. I wonder what the hell I'm going to tell Denise.

CHAPTER 19

We wait for the credits to roll. The lights come on. I thank Judy for waiting till the bitter end. "Sometimes they have funny stuff in them, like outtakes which can be funnier than the movie."

"I know!" Judy nods. "I like to watch all the credits, too. For the same reason. You just never know."

"Exactly. You never know."

We emerge a few minutes later into the crowded mall. We have half an hour to kill.

"Hey, Portia, want to do some window shopping? Or get something at the food court?"

OMG. I spy Denise, Tara, Mindy, and Randy. I open my mouth, but no words come out.

"Portia? Are you okay?"

I swallow. "Yes, I definitely could use something to drink." Thank heaven the food court is in the opposite direction.

φφφ

We buy soft pretzels and drinks. I find us a tiny table tucked into a corner where no one is likely to notice us.

I make sure to sit with my back to the wall, so I can see anyone who's approaching. I tear into my pretzel and chew like a mad cow.

"Portia, are you sure nothing's wrong?"

"I'm fine," I mumble. "Malls make me . . . anxious. All these people, you know?"

"I know what you mean," Judy says. "The crowds can make you feel claustrophobic."

"Claustrophobic. Exactly." *Why couldn't I think of that word? I'm supposed to be so smart. That's what teachers keep telling me.*

"Portia!" It's faint, but I know the voice. Maybe I'm hearing things.

"Hey, Portia!"

Oh, no. I turn my head to see Denise waving from across the food court. She's smiling. I wave back and start perspiring.

CHAPTER 20

Denise double-times over, with Mindy, Tara, and Randy bringing up the rear.

"It's great to see you, Portia!" Denise says. "I've been trying to reach you."

Her voice is neutral, without accusation. Probably doesn't want to get angry in front of this audience.

"I'm sorry," I say. "My cell phone isn't working. The battery ran down. Right now, it's out of service, as my dad would say."

Fortunately, Judy has no clue that I'm lying like a rug.

"That's okay," Denise says. "Call me later." She stabs me with a hard look.

"Of course." My cheeks burn.

"Hey, Denise. We gotta motor." Mindy points at her wristwatch. "Your mom will be waiting."

"I guess so," Denise says. She sounds reluctant. "Let's go, guys." Denise leads her entourage away.

Bringing up the rear, Randy glances at me, but says nothing.

Why is my heart pounding?

CHAPTER 21

Judy's dad drives me home. Phew. I don't have to lie (again) to Judy. I'm starting to hate this spying business. Totally. I hop out of the car and thank Mr. Lee.

φφφ

I open the front door and hear my mom talking. Either she's on the phone or with one of her friends. I close the door quietly and creep toward to the kitchen. *Sneaky me, huh?* She's on the phone. "I can't keep this up. I've talked to Mark and he won't admit what's going on."

I stop in my tracks in the hall right outside the kitchen. *She's talking about my dad. What is going on? I have to find out.*

"Every time I try to talk to him, he changes the subject," my mom says. "Mm-hmm. I know."

My mother paces past the entrance to the kitchen, turns on her heel and retreats. She turns and stares at me, hand cupped over the phone.

"Portia, how did you get home?"

I blink. "I got a ride with Judy's dad."

"Judy?" Her eyebrows draw together like magnets, and a vertical line forms between them. *If she keeps that up, her face will look like the Grand Canyon in no time.*

"You dropped me off at her house. And I had dinner there. Remember?" Annoyance colors my voice. "We went to the movies this afternoon. I was supposed to call after . . ."

My mom uncups the phone and waves her hands around. "Okay, okay, stop. I remember. Hold on a second. Wait right there." She lifts the phone to her ear. "Can I call you back? I have to go. Right now." My mom hangs up. She takes deep, even breaths, as if she's about to attempt a high dive for the Olympic gold medal.

Still clutching the receiver, she asks the phone, "How long have you been home?" *What should I say?*

CHAPTER 22

My stomach is in knots. Whether I play it straight or act dumb, I'm taking a risk.

"Portia?" My mom shifts her gaze form the phone to my face.

"Yeah?"

"You heard my question. Please answer it. How long have you been home?"

"Not long."

"What did you hear?"

"Something about how someone changes the subject when you try to talk to him."

She cocks an eyebrow. "Do you know who I was talking about?"

I shrug. "I must have missed that part."

She studies me, looking for a nervous tic or a confession. Sobbing. Pathetic.

I'm stoic. That's the word. My face is worthy of Mount Rushmore. I am a statue. And I give up nothing.

My mom nods. "Okay. Why don't you run along? I'm going to call my friend back and then start dinner."

"Mom?"

"Yes, honey?"

"Who were you talking about?"

She gasps like she's been punched in the gut. The forehead crease returns.

"Honey, please. Can we talk about this later?"

"All right."

I retreat into my bedroom and shut the door on the entire freaking world.

Throwing myself on the bed, I wonder when "later" will come.

φφφ

Time passes. I drift off. Where am I? It's foggy. I hear the ocean. Soothing. No, not ocean. Wind in the trees. Shooshing sounds. Fog rolling in. Images appear and fade out. What are they? Can't remember. They're gone the second after I see them. Ghosts. Noncorporeal. I heard that word on *Star Trek* once.

What's that noise? Off and on. Buzzing? Not quite. Bells? No. Ringing? Kind of. Annoying? Definitely grating.

I wake up with a start, drool oozing from the corner of my mouth. My cell phone jangles on the side table.

Before I can answer, it stops. With a groan, I hoist myself up and lean over to retrieve the phone and check my missed calls. And guess who it is. Denise. Well, duh!

"Ugh." I place the phone back on the table and wipe off the spit with my hand. Gross.

After a quick trip to the bathroom to splash water on my face, I return to my room, close the door and lock it. *I vant to be alone!* Where have I heard that? Ah, I remember. Greta Garbo in *Grand Hotel.* I stayed up one night to watch it with my parents on TCM. I perch on the edge of my bed and make the dreaded call to Denise.

On the second ring, she answers, "Hi, Portia. What's up?" She sounds casual. I wonder who's with her.

"Are you alone?" I ask.

"No."

"Is Randy there?"

"Uh-huh."

"Okay."

"Did you need to tell me something?"

"I . . . I got on the bus. Everything was fine. When he got off the bus, I followed him. I was trying to keep about a block away from him, so he wouldn't notice me. But then, he turned a corner. I ran to the corner and looked, but I didn't see him."

"Really?"

"I ran down the street. I saw a brick building with a wooden door. He might have gone in. Or crossed the street and disappeared."

CHAPTER 23

"I'm sorry, Denise," I say. "I guess I'm not a very good spy. I probably shouldn't be doing this at all." *Jeez! Listen to me babble!*

"Hey, don't worry," Denise says. "We'll talk tomorrow, okay?"

Her voice is calm and soothing, like Mr. Robinson's pat on the shoulder when I thought he would throw me out of the rehab clinic.

φφφ

The next day is like any Monday. I'm not looking forward to returning to school. And I'm really not looking forward to talking to Denise. I hope the calm voice I heard on the phone wasn't solely for Randy's benefit.

To top it off, my mom never told me anything more about the mystery phone call. "Later" still hasn't arrived. Obviously.

I weave my way through the crowded corridor to my locker. Kids brush by me, as if I'm not there. No one cares about me. Fine. I can take care of myself.

I open my locker, get my books, then slam it shut. I feel a tap on my shoulder. Fearfully, I steal a glance. Phew. I breathe easier when I see Judy's smile.

"Hey, Portia. I had a great time yesterday."

"Me, too."

"You want to get together for lunch?"

"I . . ." I see Denise heading straight for us. Oh, my God.

Denise strides right up, all business. "Portia, we need to talk. Let's go." She grabs my arm and starts to lead me off.

"Hold on," I say. "I was talking to my friend."

A tense moment of silence. At this point, the hallway is starting to empty. A few students are milling about. A couple of them stop and stare.

Then Denise inclines toward me and whispers in a raspy voice.

"I . . . I need a friend, too."

I glance over in complete disbelief. She's actually tearing up. The most popular girl in school says *she* needs a friend? *Am I going nuts?*

"Okay, Denise." I struggle to maintain a calm voice. "I'll talk to you in just a moment. I need to finish speaking with Judy. You interrupted us."

The kids who've stopped to listen aren't moving a muscle.

Denise nods once. "Meet me at the gym?" she asks, in a low voice.

That's familiar. That's why she yanked my arm. She wanted to talk to me alone. I'm her spy. This whole thing is supposed to be secret. So we can't be seen talking together. Of course.

But what about Mindy and Tara? I guess they don't count, huh?

CHAPTER 24

"Sure," I say. "The gym. Our usual spot?"

"Yes." Denise brightens. As I've said, she's not good at detecting sarcasm. She glances at the clock. "Uh-oh, class is starting. Gotta go. Bye!"

And off she runs.

The kids who stopped to listen all turn and look after her. Then, they look back at me.

I jut my head forward. "Boo!"

They flinch and disperse. A couple of kids give me funny looks. One girl (I would swear) is grinning.

"So," I say to Judy, "lunch sounds good. Meet you at the cafeteria later."

φφφ

I wander by the gym between first and second periods, slowing a bit, just in case. I hear a familiar *psst*. Guess who beat me there? I duck inside.

Denise reaches out and touches my arm. But she doesn't yank me under the bleachers this time. Something's changed.

"The building Randy might have entered," she says. "Did you notice what kind of building it was?"

This comes out of the blue. "No, I didn't. I'm really sorry."

"Don't worry. I have an idea," Denise says. "All you have to do is follow him again, more closely. This time, if he goes inside, follow him around. Maybe Kathleen knows someone who lives or works there, you know?"

"Denise, are you sure this is about Kathleen?" I ask. I'm starting to wonder if Denise is weirdly obsessed with the girl.

"I just have a bad feeling. You know?"

Damn. My lame attempts to end my career as a spy completely fizzle.

φφφ

The following day I'm a blonde bimbo spy again. I must switch off, so I won't be recognized. I better not run into Mr. Robinson. I tuck the brassy blonde wig under the stupid baseball cap, letting the bangs stick out in front. I have colored hair. How about that?

I repeat the routine—bike to the bus stop, hop on board the bus Randy takes. When Randy pulls the cord, I can then transfer to any bus into town and run less risk of getting caught. Assuming he keeps the same schedule, of course. And, so far, he's done the same thing every Tuesday. Maybe I'm better at spying than I think I am.

φφφ

Once again, I follow Randy to the rehab clinic. This time, I walk in right behind him, as if, by accident, we're arriving at the same time. Hide in plain sight is the idea here. I'm just a kid who happens to be here, too.

Randy signs in and says to the pretty receptionist, "How's it going?"

"Fine. Go on back."

Randy asks, "Is he feeling any better?"

The receptionist's brow puckers. "I honestly don't know. Even if I did, you know I'm not supposed to discuss patients, even in passing."

"Yeah, sure." Randy moves off.

Hmm. Randy's visiting someone. And he doesn't want to tell Denise about it. I doubt the "he" is Kathleen. I recognize Randy's tone. I've heard it in my own voice when I talk to my parents.

"Excuse me, young lady." The receptionist startles me.

"Uh, yeah?"

"Can I help you?" She smiles.

"I, uh, I . . ."

The bathroom? Again? What about Mr. Robinson?

She frowns. *Say something!* I take a deep breath. "I'm with Randy."

CHAPTER 25

The receptionist gives me a funny look, like she doesn't believe me. The corners of her mouth turn up.

"Oh, I see. Too bad he didn't introduce you. What is your name?"

"I'm, I'm Cindy." I force a wide smile. "I'm a friend from school. Would it be okay, if I joined him?" I pick up the pen, about to sign my fake name.

"Normally, it would be. However, I am surprised he didn't wait for you. That is, if you're really here together." She stabs me with a sharp look, grabs the pen from my hand and places it on the table out of my reach.

I glance past the desk and down the hall. Randy's vanished. Poof! So much for my surveillance.

φφφ

I leave the clinic, without stopping to use the restroom, although I need to. After that disastrous conversation, I may have to abort this spying gig. If the receptionist mentions me to Randy, and he tells her he doesn't know any blondes named Cindy . . . Could it be that he's cheating on Denise with a blonde named Cindy? That would be hilarious.

I head off to the bus stop. I'm disgusted and don't give a crap about anything anymore. Then it hits me: I'm not off the hook. I still have to answer to Denise. I still have a job to do. So I hang around.

My sunscreen/makeup has its limits. And hanging out on streets in seedy neighborhoods isn't good for my makeup—and it's not my idea of fun. I fit the definition of a loiterer. Go ahead, Google it.

While searching for a Starbucks, I settle for a mom-and-pop convenience store. I order a cherry Coke from a huge woman with a bulbous red nose. I wonder if her name is Rudolph.

"We have black cherry soda and Coke," she grumbles. "But no cherry Coke."

"Okay, I'll have plain Coke."

"What size?"

I pull out my money, setting aside what I need for the bus. I hand her what's left. "Whatever size this will buy me."

Slowly, the woman counts the coins. She has more trouble with math than Judy.

She shoots me a look.

"What?"

"This isn't enough for a small Coke, kid."

It sounds like an accusation. And I hate being called "kid."

The huge white lady stares down her wide red nose at me and waits. I stare back at her behind my dark glasses. I think about taking them off. Just for kicks.

"Could I have a cup of water instead?" I ask in a low voice.

"We serve water to paying customers. Buy something and I'll give you water."

I grab a pack of gum. "I'll take this and a cup of water, please."

The fat lady gives me a nasty smile. "You little smartass," she mutters, grabbing my change and ringing up the sale.

CHAPTER 26

Not feeling welcome for some reason, I hit the street. I don't want to stray too far and miss Randy leaving the clinic. I backtrack to park my sorry ass across the street where I can keep a sharp eye on the place. Midway down the block, I stop at a shop that sells collectibles and used books. Now, we're talking.

I duck inside and nose around. The musty smell of old, dusty curios and floor-to-ceiling old hardback and paperback books, permeates the place. Some books are stacked on the threadbare carpet, creating a maze. I wander through it, happily. Window shades cast a golden glow on everything. A white-haired guy with wire-rimmed glasses looks like he's sleeping at his desk. As I draw near, he looks up and says, "Hello there."

"Uh, hi."

"May I help you?"

"Just looking."

His bushy brows remind me of a ragged gray hedge.

"I didn't know anyone your age liked old stuff."

"You might be surprised."

The old guy straightens his head, and his expression relaxes into a smile. "I've lived so long, there isn't much that surprises me."

I take off my sunglasses and look at him. "You just never know."

For a moment, his smile flickers. Then, it returns full force.

"You're absolutely right."

φφφ

He tells me his name is Zack. I tell him how much I love to read and what books I've read. Zack's in the middle of telling me about a book he likes when I glance at the wall clock and realize I've been there almost an hour.

"Oh, no!"

"What's wrong?" Zack asks.

"I'm going to miss my bus."

"I'm sorry. You better run along. See you next time."

"Yeah. It was really nice talking to you." I make my way to the door. "I love talking about books. I don't get many chances to do that. I'm really glad we met. Bye."

I run at full tilt down the street thinking, I'll bet Randy is long gone. What in God's name am I going to tell Denise this time?

On my way to the bus stop, I rehearse what I'll say to Denise. A doorman wouldn't let me in. A secretary. A receptionist. Duh! Why not just tell the truth?

Because I think Randy has a reason for not telling Denise the truth. Maybe he wants to keep his visits to the clinic private.

Maybe Denise shouldn't be butting into his business at all. Which means I shouldn't be following him and telling on him, right? Or should I?

I don't owe Randy anything. Denise has invited me to her big birthday party. She's been nice to me. She even bought me a pair of cute jorts. Denise may be popular, but she seems to have problems at home. And she says she needs a friend.

This is all so confusing.

I'm at the intersection across from the bus stop. Looking both ways, I start to cross, when I feel a tap on my shoulder. I freeze. I consider ignoring it, thinking it might be a bum seeking a handout.

"Hey."

The voice behind me is male, and it sounds young.

Oh, shit.

I turn and look.

It's Randy.

I swallow. "Hey." My voice sounds like an asthmatic flute.

He squints. "You look familiar. Do I know you?"

I shake my head. "No . . . I . . . I'm Cindy."

Randy's eyes widen. "You're Cindy?" His face breaks into a grin. "Boy, Monica thought you were trying to pull a fast one on her."

For a moment, I say nothing, until I realize Monica must be the receptionist. "Oh, right. I was just curious about the place. I wasn't trying to hurt anyone. Or pull a fast one. Yeah. Ha ha."

Randy fixes me in his gaze. I'm grinning like crazy.

"Is that why you told Monica you were with me?"

"Right, right." I nod like my neck's a Slinky.

"I'd like to know why you're so curious about the place."

I grasp at mental straws.

"I have a relative who was in rehab there. I just wanted to see it." It's just a white lie. It won't hurt anyone, right?

"Really?"

I nod.

He looks down at his shoes. "Me, too. Except he's in there now."

I say nothing.

"So you know what it's like."

I nod. I hear the bus coming but stay rooted to the spot.

"That's my bus," Randy says.

"Well, what do you know. Mine, too."

"Small world."

"Yeah, right."

CHAPTER 27

"So, Cindy, there is something familiar about you," Randy
says. We're in the back of the bus. He leans against his seat
and extends his long legs. "Do you go to Jefferson Davis
Junior High?"

"I'm ... homeschooled."

I lean against the cracked-open window and gasp for air.
I'd open it wider but I fear my wig would fly off.

"Really?" Randy sits up, plants his feet on the floor and
scootches sideways. "Can I ask you something?"

Oh, God. "Sure."

"Do you get lonely?"

"All the time."

Well, it's the truth. Finally.

Randy gazes at me for a long moment.

"I believe you," he says.

Oh, shit.

What am I doing?

φφφ

"So," Randy says, "After my parents divorced, my real dad disappeared. All I ever knew was my stepfather. Everyone knows him as my dad. And all my friends think he's my dad. Even though he isn't. But I've been taught to call him Dad. Because my parents split up when I was too young to know my real father."

This information spills like water from a burst dam.

"Then I found out my real dad was a drug addict, and he'd been ordered into a rehab program."

"How'd you find that out?" I just have to ask.

"I got a copy of my birth certificate with my real dad's name on it. I went online and got the rest of the information. Easy. Anyway, I got the address of the clinic. I figured out how to get there by bus. I knew my mother would never agree to take me. From what she says about him, I can tell they didn't get along at all. I think the drugs may have caused the divorce. Maybe."

"What have you been telling your parents? Your mom and step-dad?" God knows, I could use the excuse when Denise calls.

"I just told them I've been visiting a friend I met last summer. Someone I met at summer camp."

"Does your friend have a name?" *Please, anything, but Kathleen.*

"Vince. Why?"

"Just curious." Even though I'd love to know Vince's height, weight, age, complexion, and any other distinguishing features, it might seem a bit suspicious to ask about such things.

"I chose the name Vince, because my Dad is a big fan of Vincent Price." Randy just stops. I look at him, but he won't look back at me. Two fat tears roll down his cheeks.

He backhands them. "I'm sorry. I'm acting like a big baby."

I reach out and touch his other hand. "No, you're not."

He looks at me. "Thanks, Cindy. I know we've just met, but since you've also had a relative in rehab, I feel I can trust you."

I really hate myself.

CHAPTER 28

We reach the stop and, hey, what do you know? Both of us get off at the same one. Small world, huh?

As the bus wheezes off with an awesome parting gift of toxic fumes, Randy and I make our farewells.

"Well, Cindy, it's been great talking to you."

"Yeah. Nice to meet you." I quickly unlock the chain on my bicycle.

"Look. Cindy . . ." Randy isn't making a move to leave. *Go away, Randy. I'm nothing but trouble. Believe me.*

"I hope it was okay for me to talk to you about my Dad," he says. "I really don't have anyone else."

"Gee, Randy. Don't you, um, have a best friend or something? Even a girlfriend?" I'm tucking my chain into the carryall pouch on my bike and mounting it. "You seem really nice. I'm surprised you don't have a girlfriend or best friend to talk to about this."

I'm poised to take off, when Randy's brow knits. "I'm afraid to tell them. I'm kind of worried about what they'll think. This may sound weird, but in a way, it's easier to talk to a stranger than a friend, you know?"

He looks at me and my heart melts. My foot slips off the bike pedal and hits the ground.

"Randy, can I be honest?" I say.

"Sure."

"I haven't had that many friends. So I wouldn't know."

Randy stares at me. "You're kidding."

I can't tell if Randy thinks I'm joking or saying this out of pity.

"I've moved a lot," I say. "It's hard to make friends when you move around all the time."

"Plus you're homeschooled. I forgot."

Yeah. So did I. Duh!

Randy keeps looking at me.

"Cindy, would you take off your sunglasses?"

Uh-oh.

CHAPTER 29

"I'd rather keep them on."

"Can I ask you a personal question?" he says.

"You can ask."

"Why don't you take off your glasses?"

"My eyes don't look good."

"What's wrong with them?" Randy asks.

"I've got pink eye." I can hardly keep a straight face. But the line helps to keep me from saying something I'll regret later like, "Mind your own damn business, Randy."

Is it my imagination or does Randy move back slightly? *Keep moving, Randy. You might catch something.*

Then he reaches out and briefly touches my arm. "We all hide problems, don't we?"

For once, another kid has reassured me. And it's a boy. A cute boy, at that.

I feel my face heat up. I need a cold shower. Now.

"I think I should go." I upright my bike and position myself to take off.

"Hey, Cindy." Randy places his hand on my shoulder. "I go to the rehab clinic after school every Tuesday. If you meet me, I'll be glad to make sure you get in. You can see the place, as my guest, if you like. Okay?"

I nod. "That's great. Thanks, Randy. I'll meet you at the stop or outside the clinic. Whatever. Next Tuesday. See you then."

"Wait. Let's exchange cell phone numbers. We can text each other."

"Sure."

I punch the numbers Randy recites into my phone, and he does likewise.

I roll off and wave at Randy. He waves back and walks away.

I shake my head in disbelief.

What on earth just happened?

Did I just make a date with Randy?

CHAPTER 30

I pedal straight home and go up to my room. My cell phone jangles from time to time. I ignore it. When I get to my room, I check the ID, even though I know perfectly well who it is.

Texts from Denise. *Duh!*

I perch on the edge of my bed. Okay. Deep breath.

Time to face the music.

I call Denise. This isn't a message I want to text.

Two rings and she answers. "Portia! What happened?"

"Take it easy. He didn't meet with Kathleen."

"Really? What did he do?"

"It's no big deal. I saw him hanging out with a guy."

"Oh, Portia. Are you sure?"

"Yeah, absolutely."

Well, it is the truth. Sort of.

A long silence. "Okay."

"So . . . are my spying days over?"

"I suppose . . . ."

Then, I remember how it felt when he patted my arm. That warm rush of reassurance. From a cute boy. Oh, God.

So. Not. Good.

Am I thinking about cheating on Denise with Randy?

"Portia? Are you there?"

I snap out of my dreamlike state. Who am I kidding? Randy doesn't even know me. He thinks I'm a blonde named Cindy. Ha ha ha. How stupid am I?

"Yeah, I'm here."

"What were you going to say?"

"I was just going to say that I'll do whatever you think is best."

Okay, the ball's in your court, Denise. Even if the game is rigged.

Long silence. "Let me think about it. While I have your attention, are you free this weekend?"

My first thought is to say, "Gee, Denise. Let me check my busy social calendar." But I bite my tongue. Thank God, that's just an expression or things could really get gross.

"Yeah, I am." *I think I can manage to squeeze you in.*

"Mindy and Tara are coming over Saturday afternoon. We're going to do our hair and watch movies and stuff. Want to come?"

Well, duh. "What time?"

φφφ

The week drags. By Friday, I'm more than ready for a break from these stupid kids. I miss going to a big-city school. It definitely has its benefits. Kids are bused in from all around, so it's easier to get lost in the crowd.

I'm glad I haven't seen Randy, and he hasn't seen me and noticed how much I resemble a pink-eyed blonde named Cindy who he met on the bus.

As I shuffle books in and out of my locker, Judy appears at my side, chest heaving.

"Hey, Portia."

"Hey, Judy." I assume the heaving is caused by her asthma.

"I'm really nervous."

"You are? Why's that?"

"The big quiz on Monday."

"Oh, yeah." Our teacher measures our progress from time to time. It's not as big a deal as a midterm, but it counts toward our grade. I'd forgotten about it.

"Any chance you could help me out with quadratic equations this weekend?" Judy asks.

"I . . ." I have to decide. Quickly. Will I help Judy both days or just Sunday?

What would a real friend do?

Who's to say Denise doesn't need a friend? Was she lying when she said she needed a friend? What about the problem with her mother?

Am I doing this because I really want to be her friend or just to be accepted?

And what about Randy?

I'm so confused.

But I'm not going to break my date with Denise.

"I, um, I can help you on Sunday. Would that be okay?"

Judy grins from ear to ear. "Thank you so much, Portia. You're the best."

Yeah, right.

CHAPTER 31

Saturday afternoon, a little after 2:00, I press the doorbell of the Laughton mansion. I've timed my bike ride so I get there fashionably late. I don't want to appear too anxious. Being an albino geek requires poise. Pretty cool word, huh? Poise. I read a lot of books, so I pick up a lot of cool words. If you don't know the meaning, I'm sure you'll figure it out. Or you can always Google it.

The door opens wide to reveal Denise in jeans and an oversized black tee. *What's with the shirt?* Her smile dazzles.

"Portia!" She spreads her arms and wraps me in a hug.

I grunt in response.

"It's great to see you," she says to my neck.

"Yeah."

Denise lets me go, and I can breathe again.

"C'mon in." She pulls me inside and shuts the door, before I have a chance to say anything. "My family's gone for the whole day, so it'll be just us girls."

We walk through the awesome foyer with the hypnotic crystal chandelier. I keep my eyes averted from it, like Ulysses ignoring the Sirens (and if you haven't seen that movie where Michael Douglas's dad, Kirk, plays Ulysses, you should—it's awesome), although I can't resist taking a quick sneak peek. Just that one glimpse gives me the chills, as if I've committed a terrible sin. What is it about that fixture? It reminds me of that mythic creature with snakes for hair. What's her name? You turn to stone if you look at her. Ah, Medusa. That's it.

"Hey, Portia. You want a Coke or something?"

"Huh?" I realize we're standing in the kitchen. It's freaking huge, roughly the size of Judy's entire first floor.

"Yeah, I'd like a Coke, please," I say, landing with a thud on one of the ladder-back chairs clustered around the solid-looking wood table in the glassed-in breakfast nook that juts into a lush landscape of palm trees, gladiolas, hibiscus, tall grasses, and other ornamental trees, shrubs, and flowers.

Denise grabs two glasses, fills them with ice from a fancy dispenser and then pours Coke—slowly so it doesn't run over.

What's wrong with this picture?

I've never seen Denise wear an oversized tee. Let alone in *black*. I've only seen Denise in girlie colors, like pink and violet. Or yellow. She hands me my glass. The house is totally silent.

"Denise, where is everyone?"

My words come out in a rush.

Denise sits next to me. She looks at her lap and heaves a sigh. "I asked you to come early, because I wanted to talk to you alone. There are things I can't talk about with anyone else. I feel like I can trust you."

I stare at her. "Me? What about your friends?"

And do you realize I have a date with your boyfriend? Maybe.

Then, the most amazing thing happens. Denise's mouth crumples. Tears stream down her cheeks. She looks up at me. "Portia. I don't have any real friends."

I'm stunned. "What about Mindy and Tara?"

"Yeah. What about them?"

For a moment, I'm at a loss for words.

"But they're like your BFFs, right?"

Denise laughs, but she doesn't sound happy.

"BFFs? Best friends forever? Hardly. Best friends for as long as they need me."

My blood runs cold. I realize I'm spying on Randy because I want Denise to accept me. Am I any different from Mindy and Tara?

Then, Denise blows me away by saying, "Portia, you're so smart. I wish I could be more like you."

CHAPTER 32

Okay, enough of this crazy talk.

"You're kidding. You have no idea what it's like to be me."

" Portia, you're so smart. And you're good at everything."

"That's ridiculous," I say. Now I'm getting pissed. Denise may mean well, but she has no idea what she's talking about. "Why on earth would you want to be like me? I'm a colorless freak. I have no friends."

"What about that girl you were with the other day?"

"What?"

"The black girl. She was at the mall with you. Obviously, you guys are real tight."

"Oh, Judy." I think about our brief encounter at the mall. "What makes you think we're so tight?"

Denise pauses and stares out the window at the garden. "When I saw you at the locker, you wouldn't walk away from her, just because I wanted to talk to you. Real friends are there for each other. You stayed there for her.

"If push came to shove, I don't think Mindy or Tara would do that for me. They only hang with me because they think I'm cool and they want everyone to think they're cool, too."

I'm too astonished to say a word. Is this some sort of game? Or is Denise just crazy? Whatever it is, I am losing patience. "Look, Denise. You're the most popular girl at school. You're pretty and blonde and perfect in every way. Everyone freaking loves you. You live in a palace. Haven't you noticed the diamond chandelier hanging in your foyer? You even have a boyfriend. And whatever he's doing, he's not cheating on you. You wear nice clothes. Everything in your life is perfect. Why can't you just be happy?"

My words explode.

Denise turns to look at me and bursts into tears.

"Thanks. You sound just like my mother."

Her mother. I'd totally forgotten. I'm such an idiot.

CHAPTER 33

Denise is sobbing so hard, she starts hiccupping. I get up and hug her. This isn't normal behavior for me, so I feel clumsy. Yet, it feels like the right thing to do.

"I'm sorry," I say. The words come quite easily. Probably because it's the truth. I don't have a problem saying true things, even if they suck. Most of the time, people have a hard time hearing them. I don't say the true things often enough, because no one wants to hear them.

This spying business has been hard, because I must keep lying. And I hate lying. Someone once said that if you told the truth all the time, you wouldn't have to worry, because it was a whole lot less work than remembering all those lies and trying to keep them straight. Something like that, anyway.

So, I keep hugging Denise. I have no idea what else to say or do.

"Portia. Please let go."

I release her.

She gasps. "Thanks." Her chest heaves. For a moment, I think of Judy.

"Wow, you're strong, for a small girl," Denise says.

"I am?"

This is news.

"Do you work out or something?"

"Are you kidding? The heaviest things I lift are books."

Denise smiles. "I'll bet you've picked up some really big books, huh?"

Where is this conversation going?

"Um, yeah."

"See that's what I'm talking about. My mother would love you." Denise stops and stares at her lap.

There it is again. Denise's mother. I think back to when I met her in the car going to the mall. The way Denise recoiled when her mom tried to give her a quick peck on the cheek. I assumed she didn't want to be treated like a kid in front of her friends. I can relate.

Then, later in her room, she nearly took my head off when I mentioned her mom. That's when I knew there was something seriously wrong lurking inside this pretty house.

Now, the house is so quiet, all I hear is my blood roaring in my ears. Denise keeps staring at her lap. I'm trying to figure out how to ask what's wrong with her mother without causing her to pitch a fit.

But I'm definitely not raising the subject of Randy. Not yet.

CHAPTER 34

There's a delicate balance between us that I'm afraid to disturb by talking. But someone has to speak, because we can't let this silence go on forever.

"Denise, is there something you want to tell me?"

It's all I can think of saying that won't give anything away.

Denise looks up. Her eyes search my face. The doorbell rings. Her expression collapses into disappointment.

"That must be Mindy and Tara," she says. She sounds like they've come to pull out her teeth.

She rises and goes to answer the door.

The three girls come into the kitchen. Mindy and Tara are dressed in jeans and loose-fitting Ts. Just like Denise. I guess she's their fashion consultant. She ought to charge them. Ha ha.

Denise is smiling and laughing now. As if nothing had happened before the girls arrived. *What's up with that?*

Mindy sees me and stops short. Tara nearly collides with her.

"Guys, you remember Portia, right?" Denise sounds almost giddy.

Mindy's gaze is fixed on me. "You didn't mention she'd be here," she says in a low voice.

I can hear you plain as day. And what's your problem? We all got along just fine at the mall last week. Remember?

"Does it matter?" Denise says. "We had so much fun at the mall, I figured it would be great to get together today and hang out here."

As Denise babbles, Mindy keeps staring at me.

"So …" Denise claps her hands. "What would you guys like to do? Watch a movie? Make popcorn? What?" Tara's head emerges from behind Mindy. "I thought it might be fun to streak our hair, then watch a movie. How about you three?"

Denise's eyes widen to dinner-plate size. "Ooh. Streak our hair? What color?"

Tara rifles through a plastic shopping bag and removes two boxes. "Blue or purple?"

"Oh. My. Gawd." Denise comes down hard on each word. "That would drive my mother crazy."

Guess what we're doing this afternoon.

CHAPTER 35

We color our hair and watch a goofy comedy while our hair dries. If my life depended on it, I couldn't tell you the title. But it makes me laugh.

We make popcorn. What we don't eat, we throw at each other. When the movie's over, Denise says we should go, before her parental units return, because it won't be pretty when they see her hair. Or the popcorn strewn around the living room.

"Need any help cleaning up?" I ask.

"Nah. We've got a cleaning lady. She'll take care of it."

For a moment, I wonder if the cleaning lady is black or Hispanic. But I bite my tongue. Again. *Ouch.*

Tara and Mindy, who live only a couple of blocks away, make for the door.

"Think your parents will flip out?" Mindy asks, pointing to Tara's purple-streaked locks.

"Nah. They'll be fine. I guess." Tara looks thoughtful, then smiles. "How about yours?"

"Mine are cool. No problemo." Mindy runs her fingers through her purple-tinted hair.

"It was great to see you, Portia." Tara smiles and waves.

"Great to see you guys, too." I wave back at them.

Mindy echoes. "Yeah, same here."

I hang back as the two girls leave. Denise is picking up popcorn.

"Are you sure you don't need help?" I ask. *And I don't mean cleaning up.*

Denise stops and looks me in the eye. "Why would I need your help? I have everything I need, right?"

Oh, shit. The balance between us was disturbed when the other girls came in.

Looks like I've blown it. "Well, I guess I better go then," I say, turning toward the door.

"Hey, Portia."

"Yeah?" I stop and look back at Denise.

"Thanks for coming by early. And thanks for listening." Denise smiles. "Your hair looks nice, by the way."

"Oh," I pat my head, self-consciously. "My parents are probably going to be, um, surprised."

"Tell them I insisted. Your friend, Denise, said you needed a little color to bring out the natural beauty of your features."

She pronounces the words like an expert in an infomercial. We snicker at the ridiculousness.

"Really, though," she adds. "You look awesome."

For a moment, I don't trust myself to answer. I feel so happy, I may lose it. Then, I realize Denise is probably just being polite. How lame would it be to get all weepy because another kid was nice to you? So, I pull myself together and muster an appropriate response, without getting all emo over it.

"Thanks, Denise. So do you."

She pauses. "You know, Portia. Coming from you, I actually believe that."

Good, because it's actually the truth. That's what I want to say, but don't.

I leave and hop on my bike. I realize we never discussed Randy. And I haven't returned the blonde spy outfit. I shrug. Oh, well. Later, right?

On the ride home, I ponder explanations for my hair being streaked with blue. Same color as Denise's.

CHAPTER 36

When I get home, Mom's in her usual dither. On the phone, not happy with this thing or that.

"Hi, Mom," I say, waving.

Her jaw slackens. "I . . . Can I call you back?" She disconnects and drops the phone.

"What have you done with your hair?" she shrieks.

Well, I guess that got her attention. Finally.

"Why? Don't you like it?"

"Well . . . it's different."

"So, you don't like it."

"I didn't say that."

"Whatever." I turn and start walking away.

"Portia."

Something in her voice makes me stop cold. I turn to look at her. My Mom is staring at me.

I steel myself. "What is it?"

She shakes her head. "What's going on? Why'd you do that to your hair?"

"Why shouldn't I? It's my hair."

"Well, of course, but . . ."

A silent moment stretches for eons. The kitchen clock ticks.

"Can I go to my room now?" I ask.

My Mom takes a deep breath, as if she's doing yoga. "Of course. Your father and I will want to talk to you later about . . . this." She touches her own hair. She actually means mine.

"Fine. Whatever." I want this conversation to end.

"Portia, wait." This time, her voice makes my heart melt. She seems to be on the verge of tears.

I harden inside. *Don't cry. You're not a child.*

"Now what?" I ask.

She shakes her head. "You're growing up so fast. That's all."

She smiles and leans down to hug me. I hug her back tightly, but I think, *This can't be just about my hair.*

"Mom, is something wrong?" I mumble into her neck.

"I'm a bit tired," she says. "And you surprised me. I wasn't expecting you to come home with blue-streaked hair." She pulls away and grins.

I return her grin, but I wonder if there's more to the story.

Later, my Dad comes home and we all sit down to dinner. He takes one look at me and raises an eyebrow. My parents exchange glances, which I choose to ignore. They make meaningless chitchat about their day and ask me about mine, without mentioning the hair. After dinner, I rinse off the dishes and load the dishwasher. My Dad comes into the kitchen.

"Hey, kiddo. Got a minute? Your Mom and I have something we'd like to discuss with you."

I finish up, wipe the counter, dry my hands and go to the living room for our big discussion. "My goodness," Dad says. "That color is quite . . ."

I fill in the blank. "Different?"

"Exactly! Blue is a very different color for hair. Don't you think?"

So is nothing. Having hair that's no color is even more different. But how would you know?

My Mom chimes in. "What prompted this? Did the other girls talk you into this?"

"Other girls?" My Dad looks from Mom to me with curiosity. He doesn't have a clue about my social life. At least Mom knows I've got a few friends. *Yes, Dad! Amazing, but true.*

How can I explain that all I want to do is have fun and be part of the group. Just be a normal kid doing kid stuff. Like playing catch with popcorn or dying hair. But they don't seem to understand. It's like I colored my hair intentionally to provoke them. I just wanted to do it. That's all.

I try to explain in terms I hope they'll understand. They're parents, not kids. They've forgotten what it's like.

"I just wanted to do something different and interesting. You know? Ever feel that way? Like life was dull and you needed to do something more?"

My Dad looks puzzled. "You're too young to sound so jaded." He chucks me under the chin. "Smile, things aren't that bad, are they?"

My Mom looks at me, her eyes bright. She keeps silent.

CHAPTER 37

The next day, I pedal to Judy's to help her with math. I'm
thinking about how grim things looked last night during our
big talk. I wondered at one point if they were going to
ground me. Fortunately, they didn't.

I've never been grounded. I've always been the good,
reliable kid. Good grades, no trouble, everything a parent
would want in a child. Except, of course, having zero social
skills. Until recently. I'm beginning to wonder about these
people I've been living with who claim to be my parents.
They don't even look like me. Who are they to tell me how
to live, anyway? Don't I have rights? Don't my opinions
matter?

I pedal faster and faster. I arrive at Judy's house nearly out
of breath. I lean my bike against the side of the house, creak
up the steps and rap on the door. Judy answers, looking
frantic.

"I'm so worried about this quiz, Portia." She squints at
me. "Why did you dye your hair?"

"You don't like it?"

"It's . . . different."

"Yeah. So I've been told. You don't like it?"

"No, no. I didn't mean that. I'll get used to it."

"Sure." I feel my face grow hot. Am I angry at Judy or myself for dying my hair blue.

"C'mon in. Let's get started."

Judy's mom appears with a bright smile. "Hi, Portia," she says. Either she doesn't notice my hair or is too polite to comment. "Would you like something to drink?"

"Sure, Mrs. Lee. Do you have any more of that lemonade?"

She nods. "Sure thing. How about you, honey?"

"Okay, Mom. Thanks." Waiting for my lemonade, I listen to the homey sounds of the refrigerator door opening and closing with a *thunk,* ice rattling into glasses, liquid splashing. Mrs. Lee comes in cradling a full glass of lemonade in each hand.

"Here you go, girls. Now, don't study too hard."

I notice Marmalade creeping toward us. "Hey, there's your cat," I say.

"Oh, her," Judy says. "We can play with her later."

"I just want to . . . let her know I'm sorry. About stepping on her tail."

Judy waves her hand. "She's already forgotten, I'm sure."

I squat down and extend a hand toward the orange cat. "Hey, Marmalade. Here, kitty kitty." I keep my voice low and soothing.

Marmalade looks at me with golden eyes. They seem to look right through me.

"I'm sorry, Marmalade. I didn't mean to hurt you," I whisper.

The cat looks at me as if to say, *You're not fooling me one bit.* Then she turns and saunters off.

Why do I feel so guilty?

φφφ

After a couple of hours of repetitive math exercises, I insist we take a short break. Judy is catching on slowly. Going over the material an extra day wouldn't have hurt. But I'm not responsible for that, am I? I'm entitled to a life, right?

I wished Judy had studied on her own while I was dying my hair and going to a movie.

"Hey, want to take another crack at Happy Hamster?" Judy asks.

I shrug. "Sure." That's what I need to pick me up. The sound of a hamster drowning. Repeatedly.

Judy hits the remote. She hits another button and the screen goes blue. Hey, it almost matches my hair.

"There," she says, as the images pop up on the screen. "Want to go first?"

"Okay." May as well drown and be done with it.

With the controller, I go through what are now familiar motions. A series of leaps, hops, and rides. I repeat the routine several times. My hamster arrives at the water hazard. The crumbling cliff always gets me. I land too close to the edge and tumble into the water. Unable to retreat to solid land, I go down gurgling, helpless. Again and again.

Judy roots for me. "C'mon, Portia." Time your jump so you land as far from the edge as you can. You can do it."

Wait a minute. Doesn't she want to win? We're supposed to be competing.

For a moment, I feel a wave of shame and anger. *Don't pity me.*

Next time I hit the remote so the hamster hops onto a bee that flies up to a swinging platform. I hit the button again and he lands on the platform. Barely. He (or is it she?) teeters a bit, but holds on. The platform rises higher and higher. A rainbow comes into view. At this point, I prepare to hit the button so the hamster can jump onto the rainbow and slide down into the pot of gold.

But first, I must pass the water hazard. This means I have to leap onto the ground past the crumbling cliff. Can I time the jump right?

Not me, of course. I'm talking about the hamster. And, I keep forgetting, this is just a game. A silly game.

Okay, here comes the cliff. Now or never. I hold my breath, hit the button, and pray. I don't even believe in God, but I pray.

The hamster jumps and lands. "Yay! I did it!" I yell.

"I knew you could." Judy is all smiles. She gives me a high five. "Nice!"

I've been holding my breath and my shoulders are hunched. I exhale and my whole body relaxes. "I can't believe it."

"Just a matter of practice," Judy says, all matter of fact. "And it's much more fun against a real player."

CHAPTER 38

Monday rolls around. We take the math quiz. Judy feels like she might have done okay, but not great. I feel bad about not going over to her house on Saturday. Then I remind myself that she could have spent time studying on her own. I hope she does okay on the quiz.

In the next few days, I'm getting attention from other kids. They're noticing me. This puzzles me—and then it hits me like a ton of bricks. It's because of the blue streaks in my hair. *Oh, my God! They think* I'm *making a fashion statement.* I find this absolutely hilarious.

φφφ

Judy and I sit together at lunch again. "I was thinking," Judy says. "Do you want to come over again? Or . . ."

I'm picking at my mystery meat. "Or what?"

No answer.

"Do you want to come over to my house?" She doesn't hear or she's ignoring me. "Why don't you want to come over?"

She points to something behind me.

Uh-oh. I turn to look. Sure enough, the popular kids are huddled around their table. Denise is a stand-out with her electric blue-streaked hair. Mindy and Tara, pretty in purple, flank her. I can't seem to locate Randy. Could be I'm not looking hard enough. Or maybe he's not at school today. Who knows?

Judy's expression is a huge question mark.

"Is that what you were doing on Saturday?" she asks.

She doesn't sound angry or accusatory. But I still feel terrible.

"I'm sorry. Denise invited me over before you asked me to help you study. I didn't want to . . . disappoint her."

She nods. "It's okay." She refuses to make eye contact. *No. You don't understand. I'm spying for Denise, but no one can know that. Not even you. I'm sorry. I'm so sorry.*

I glance over at Denise. She's laughing it up with her friends. She won't look at me. *That's because no one's supposed to know we're friends. Except Mindy and Tara, I guess. Denise must have sworn them to secrecy because they're not looking at me, either.*

Then it hits me. Mindy and Tara know I'm friendly with Denise, but they don't know why.

And neither does Judy.

"Well," Judy says. "I'm going to go to the library." She grabs her tray and starts to get up.

"Wait. Please. Don't go." I latch onto Judy's arm. "There's something I need to tell you."

Judy looks at me, her liquid brown eyes filled with concern. She sits down. "What's wrong, Portia?" *Whoa!* Someone actually cares.

"You're the only real friend I have here. If I can't trust you with a secret, I don't know who I can trust. So I'm going to tell you something, but you have to promise not to tell anyone, okay?"

"Of course, Portia. What is it?"

"You swear you won't tell anyone? On pain of death? On your mother's grave? On a stack of Bibles? Whatever."

Judy shakes her head. "Wow. That must be quite a secret. I'd never betray a friend's secret. And you're my only friend here, too. Which is why I was a little disappointed when you said you were at Denise's on Saturday. But I also understand it's important to keep your promises. Besides, everyone can have other friends. Especially popular girls like Denise."

I wave my hand to cut her off. "It's not just because Denise is popular."

Really, it isn't?

"There's a favor I'm doing for her."

"Oh?" Judy eyebrows draw together. "What kind of favor?"

"Let's go someplace a bit more private, and I'll fill you in."

CHAPTER 39

We retreat to the girl's restroom and check the stalls to be sure they're unoccupied. Then I give Judy a quick rundown, leaving out the part about how I might be cheating on Denise with her boyfriend. Because I'm not really sure that I am cheating.

Judy's eyes widen. "So the most popular girl in school needs your help. And she doesn't want anyone to know. Why?"

"Exactly."

"And you're spying on her boyfriend in exchange for her promise to be friends with you?"

Her voice seems to mock me. Judy may not be good at math, but she's a quick study when it comes to people.

"Uh, yeah."

"How about Randy? What have you found out about him?"

Now what do I say? I've promised Randy to keep his secret. I can't betray him. But I don't want to lose Judy's trust, either. Being a spy is way more complicated than I expected.

"I'm sorry. I'm sworn to absolute secrecy on that."

Judy peers at me. "I'm not trying to be mean, but didn't you just give away Denise's secret?"

"Well, yeah, but only because I trust you."

"But you don't trust me with this other secret?"

Well, she had me there. With no idea what to say, I shut the hell up.

Judy started in again. "Why aren't you telling me everything?"

"You'd make a great interrogator," I shot back.

"Portia." Judy's eyes radiate concern. "Are we really friends?"

Without hesitation, I reply. "Yes." I grasp her arms and look her straight in the eyes. If that sounds weird, like we are lovers, too bad. I'm not gay, but I don't care what the world thinks.

"Then, there's some reason you're not telling me the whole truth, even though you trust me with Denise's secret."

Nice going, Judy. If logic doesn't work, play the guilt card.

"Here's the thing, Judy. This problem Denise thinks she has doesn't exist. So I don't feel bad for her. But this other secret, if it were to get out that I told someone, even by mistake, I'd feel really terrible."

Judy keeps silent.

"Judy, remember when you told me about how your phone was disconnected?"

"Huh? What's that have to do with this?"

"I told you I wouldn't tell anyone, and I meant it. The same thing applies to this secret, okay?"

Judy nods, and her sad expression turns into a smile. "Spying must be hard. I would hate to have to keep all those secrets. That's a lot of work. If you ever want to talk, I'm a good listener. That's what friends are for, right?"

φφφ

Even though I've assured Denise that Randy is not seeing Kathleen, I've agreed to follow Randy again. Denise doesn't know about my ulterior motive—um, date. I still have the blonde spy outfit. I bought my own bottle of makeup with sunscreen. After school, I sneak into the restroom of a fast-food joint and get all dressed up. At the bus stop a short time later, I secure my bike to the lamppost and pull out my cell phone. Randy has texted me: *C U soon.* My heartbeat quickens. Three silly little words. Okay, one word and two letters. Whatever.

I've left my backpack at home. I prefer to travel light, but I wish I had a book to pass the time. With nothing to read I think about what I'll say to Randy when he steps off the bus. I'm pacing because I'm so wired. I check to see if I've left a groove in the sidewalk. Why am I so nervous? He's just a guy. A cute guy who seems to like me. Maybe he likes me only in a blonde wig with dark glasses. That's the thing, isn't it? Does he really like *me?*

The bus pulls up. Randy gets off. He looks over and waves. "Hi, Cindy."

"Hi, Randy."

"Hey, you look great," he says with a smile.

I smile back, feeling like the fraud I am. "Thanks." He looks so cute. Like Justin Bieber with a crooked nose.

The express bus arrives.

"So, what's your story?" Randy asks as we file on.

"Huh?"

"I was just wondering why you were visiting the rehab center. But it's really not my business." Randy looks away. "I'm sorry. I didn't mean to pry."

Now what do I do? Tell the truth or come up with another lie?

CHAPTER 40

As we head down the highway, I stare out the window, thinking. Always thinking. Randy may think I'm stoned or ignoring him. I need to say something. Now.

His head is bent over a book.

"Randy."

"Yes?" His eyes meet mine.

"I . . . wanted to say, I consider you a friend."

He nods. "Same here."

"I want you to know that whatever happens, I've never intended to hurt anyone."

"Cindy, why would you even say that?"

Okay, how do I play this? Whose trust should I betray?

I let out a shaky breath. "Well, first of all, my name's not Cindy."

"Really? What's your name?"

"Portia." I utter it with disdain.

Randy looks thoughtful. "Portia. That's a nice name. Isn't Portia a character in a Shakespeare play?"

"Yeah." This surprises me. Randy's more than just a cute guy. He has a brain. This makes it even harder to tell him the whole truth.

"Wasn't she smart?"

"Right."

"So why do you go by Cindy?" He wrinkles his nose.

"I . . . don't like my name that much. What's wrong with Cindy?"

He shakes his head. "Nothing. But it's not . . . I don't know how to say it."

"Interesting?"

"Yeah. Interesting. That's a good word."

"I seem to excel at being interesting."

Randy smiles. "What's that supposed to mean?"

"Well," I say, pausing to choose my words. "I'm not a blonde."

Randy laughs. "You dye your hair? So what? Lots of chicks do. Big deal."

Yeah, Randy, I dyed my hair. But I didn't dye it blonde.

"Actually, it's a wig."

"Really?" His eyes widen. "It looks so real. Can I touch it?"

"Sure. Go ahead."

He reaches out and massages a strand of my fake hair between finger and thumb. As he does, his hand caresses my cheek.

"Wow, it feels real. Why are you wearing a wig?" His hand flies to his mouth. "Please tell me it isn't because you've had cancer."

If Randy didn't look so horrified, I'd laugh. "No, I haven't had cancer."

"Oh, thank God. I thought maybe that was why you were being homeschooled. Like maybe you were too sick from chemo to attend school."

Funny. Everyone knows about cancer and how horrible it is. But nobody knows what I'm going through. If I had cancer, someone could *do* something to get rid of it. Or I'd die. But no doctor or miracle worker can do anything to change who I am. I'm a colorless albino freak. And I always will be. If I were a cancer kid, people would care. But I'm just invisible.

That's when I make my decision. Randy has to accept me as I am. And I can't stay silent forever. Not if we're really friends.

"Hey, here's our stop." Randy reaches up and pulls the cord.

Saved by the bell. For now.

CHAPTER 41

I've heard that timing is everything. It is. Randy drops the subject of my hair.

We stroll through the crappy neighborhood toward the rehab center, like we're a couple of kids going on our way to buy groceries.

"So, Cindy . . . I mean, uh, Portia. If you were visiting someone, how come you didn't sign in?"

Oh, shit. How can I protect Denise and keep Randy's confidence?

"Randy. I wasn't visiting anyone. I just needed to get inside."

Randy peers at me. "Why?"

"Because I was curious."

Still true. Not the whole truth, but still true.

Randy halts. "What's going on?"

"What do you mean?"

"You're wearing a wig and trying to sneak into a rehab center because you're curious." He smiles, but his voice hardens. "Are you training for the CIA?"

Oh, double-shit. I think it's time to face the music.

"Randy, you do consider me a friend, right?"

"I do. Even though we've just met, you seem nice and very smart."

"Okay." I pause and take a breath. "I need to show you something."

Randy nods.

"Promise me you won't freak out."

"Portia, what is it?"

I remove the cap and wig. Randy stares at my blue-streaked white hair.

"Haven't I seen you before?"

I nod. "Probably at school." I remove the dark glasses. "I'm the one who has pink eye. Two of them. Remember?"

I laugh my stupid little joke. To my great surprise Randy laughs with me. Thank God.

Before I know it, I'm feeding Randy more bull about how I was curious about where he was going. It was my idea to dress up and follow him to the rehab center. I want to keep Denise's name out of the whole thing.

"And then we met and got to know each other. And I didn't know how to tell you. I don't have many friends, because I've moved so many times—and because my appearance scares people. I'm always the strange albino chick, the freak.

"When you told me on the bus about your dad, I could sympathize. Sometimes I need to talk to someone, too. And sometimes I feel like my parents aren't really there for me. Know what I mean?"

We're approaching the rehab center. Randy doesn't interrupt or get angry. He just listens and nods. I'm surprised, because I'm rambling. I think I would have hauled off and slugged myself by now.

We pause.

"Well, Randy," I say. "I'll go home now. Thanks for listening—and being my friend." It's all I can do to keep from crying.

"Wait." He places his hand on my arm. "Why are you leaving?"

My jaw drops. "I . . . figured you'd hate me."

Randy stares at me. "Are you kidding?"

My face grows hot. I feel like an idiot. And I have no clue, as usual. "You mean, you're not angry at me for lying and following you?"

Randy moves closer. "I understand why you lied. And I know exactly how you feel. I haven't told anyone but you that I come here to see my real father, because I'm afraid to tell anyone else."

CHAPTER 42

"I can't believe you're not angry with me. I'm angry with me!" He holds the door and we go in. Randy shakes his head. "You're hopeless, but you're all right for a girl."

Whoa! That's almost a compliment.

I follow Randy to the receptionist's desk. She is still pretty. And I can't remember her name to save my life.

Having no reason for a disguise, I've stuffed the itchy blonde wig in my backpack and tucked my blue-streaked hair under my ball cap. For the moment, dark glasses still cover my pink eyes.

"Hi, Monica," Randy says. "This is my friend, Portia. She's my guest today."

Monica's gazes at me. I see recognition in her eyes.

I fake a laugh. "Hi, Monica. Remember me?"

Monica's face looks pinched. "Isn't your name Sandy?"

"Nope."

You must have me mistaken for a really stupid liar. Randy steps in. "Oh, that. That was my mistake. Portia looks like a girl I know named Cindy. When I mentioned Cindy, I was wrong. It was really Portia."

Monica looks incredulous. The corners of her mouth turn up slightly. "I see."

I'll bet.

φφφ

We sign in. I follow Randy down the hall and bump into Mr. Robinson leaving his office.

"Hello, Randy."

Randy turns and waves. "Hey, Mr. Robinson."

I'm ready to have a heart attack.

"Who's your friend?" Mr. Robinson asks.

Keep going, Randy. Please keep going. "This is Portia, my friend from school."

"Really?" I turn and look up at him. He's very tall and he's wearing that same old brown suit again. "My, my. Your name is Portia? We weren't properly introduced last time, were we?"

I shake my head. "No, sir."

Mr. Robinson chuckles. "You should have told me you knew Randy from school. I know some of Randy's friends. One in particular I know quite well."

I look at Randy who shrugs.

"Mr. Robinson," Randy says. "I have to go now. It's nice to see you."

"Nice to see you, too, Randy. And you, Portia." Great big smile.

"Nice to meet you, Mr. Robinson." I bare my teeth at him.

CHAPTER 43

We meet Randy's father in the glass-enclosed sunroom. It reminds me of an aquarium without water. The floor is covered with wall-to-wall gray carpeting. There's a conversation pit with a worn brown Naugahyde sofa. A blue-and-white afghan is draped over one arm. Two matching chairs flank the sofa. Metal folding chairs and small tables fill the room. I count one plant, a potted ficus in the corner. A man gets up from the sofa and greets Randy. I expected a bedridden old coot. *Boy, am I ever wrong.*

He opens his arms to his son. "Randy, good to see you."

"Hey, Dad." Randy wraps his arms around his father. I've never before seen two men embrace.

I suppose I've seen too many *From Drugs to Mugs* movies at school. Randy's father is nothing like that. He is tall and slender with brown hair. There is a strong resemblance between father and son.

Randy steps back but doesn't let go. "Dad, this is Portia. She's a really good friend from school."

There's an odd tone in Randy's voice. A hint of apology?

Randy's father smiles at me. "Any friend of Randy's is a friend of mine." He offers me a hug.

I accept, but I'm so shocked, I can't even manage to say, "It's nice to meet you."

"Let's sit down and talk," he says "How about something to drink. We have soda, water, or juice."

I follow Randy's lead. He wants an orange soda. I've never been a fan, but today I want an orange soda, too. Randy's dad asks about school, what he's doing for fun. You know, the usual stuff. Father and son have a shy, intelligent, manner—a winning combination in my book.

His dad turns to me. "I'm sorry. I didn't mean to ignore you, Portia."

"Huh?" I'm so used to being ignored, I hadn't even noticed.

"You and Randy. Good friends, huh?" He winks and smiles.

I glance at Randy. His mouth is hanging open. He blushes and shrugs.

I bristle. "Yes, we're *just* friends," I say, dripping sarcasm. *Damn. I didn't mean to do that."* Randy's dad stops smiling. I stare at my lap and wish I really was invisible.

Randy laughs but it's phony. He's a poor actor. "Portia's feeling a little down today," he says. I look up at Randy and he smiles at me. Encouraging.

"I'm sorry," I say to Randy's father. I didn't mean any disrespect."

"That's quite all right," he says. "I know what it's like to feel so bad you get angry at the slightest provocation. Is that how you feel?"

"Well . . ." Wait a minute. When did this visit become about me? Randy's nodding, egging me on like I should say something. "I don't want to bore you with my problems. Please just ignore me."

"Okay. But when you're feeling bad, sometimes it helps to talk about it. I know." Randy's father leans toward me and bathes me in the warmth of his gaze. "Just think about it."

I nod. I don't trust myself to say a word.

"May I ask you something, Portia?"

"What?" I manage to say.

"Why are you wearing sunglasses?"

"Oh." I'm so used to hiding behind them, I forget they're on. "Well, I'm . . ."

Randy's father waits patiently for my reply.

"I . . ." I can't seem to find the word, so I just pull off the glasses and look at him.

I can tell by the change in his expression that my appearance has shocked him. "I didn't realize . . ." he begins to say.

"That I have pink eye?" I can't help myself and I burst out laughing. Randy and his dad laugh along with me. And that feels great.

CHAPTER 44

The wall clock tells me it's time to leave. Randy's father walks us to the door. He gives Randy one last hug then turns to me.

"Portia," he says. "Feel free to come by anytime to talk. Anytime you like." He hugs me.

As we leave the building, I think about Zack, the guy who sells the used books. I want to tell him who I really am. He knows me as a redhead. I just know I want to talk to Zack, wearing my real hair. "Randy, I'd like to stop at the bookstore across the street. They sell old books and stuff."

Randy smiles. "I like old books. We can hang out for a while. But not too long, because I need to get home for dinner."

"Thanks, Randy." I'm smiling like crazy. I remember Denise and feel terrible. But what does Randy see in Denise? I would ask, but I'm afraid. We cross the street and step inside the shop. The place is as cluttered as when I was here before. And it is still dusty. I adjust to the dim light and look around. No Zack.

"Hello?"

A slim woman with long, dark hair emerges from the back. "Hello. I'll be with you in a moment," she says.

She disappears. Randy and I exchange looks. I wonder where Zack is. Who's this lady? His daughter? She seems much too young to be his wife.

Of course, who am I to judge anyone else? I spied on Randy in order to befriend Denise. In the process, I developed a crush on him. What kind of friend does that?

The woman reappears and walks over. "Hi there. Sorry to keep you waiting. How may I help you?"

"I was hoping to see Zack," I say. *And who are you?*

"Were you a regular customer?"

"I only met him once, but he was so friendly." *And why are we talking about him as if we were at his funeral?*

The woman blinks and rubs her eyes. A few tears run down her cheeks. "I'm sorry. This is difficult. I'm Zack's granddaughter. Zack died yesterday morning. Our family is getting ready to close the store."

"Oh, no . . ." My voice trails off. I scan the shop, hoping Zack will appear from behind a stack of books. This can't be happening.

"We have to close the store. Business has been off for some time. My grandpa kept it going because he loved it."

My voice is a whisper. "I just met him," I say. "I can't believe he's gone." The woman touches my shoulder. "Honey, I know it's hard. But it's part of life. Things get old. People grow old and eventually die. There's no escape."

CHAPTER 45

"I know people die," I say. "I'm not *that* dumb. Leave me alone." I run out the door, slamming it behind me. When I reach the corner, I realize I've left Randy behind.

I stand there feeling stupid and waiting for the feeling to go away. It's like a fog that won't lift. I want to cry, but the tears won't come. Funny, I met Zack once. I hardly knew him. But he made an impression on me. And he was one of the few people I could talk to about books..

My whole life seems like a terrible dream, and I want to wake up.

I feel a tap on my shoulder. I look back and Randy is peering at me.

"Are you okay?" he asks.

"I'll live," I say, not answering his question.

"I'm . . . sorry." He places his hand on my arm.

I turn around and face him. "Don't worry. It's not your fault he died. People die all the time."

"Look, I only meant . . ."

"I know. You feel sorry for me. Don't worry about it. Life sucks and that's just the way it is. Old books and old things and old people don't matter. Everything dies. Who cares?"

"Portia, stop it!" he shouts.

The fog lifts. I realize I'm acting like a jerk. "I . . . I'm sorry, Randy."

Randy takes a deep breath. "It's okay, Portia. I understand. I'm your friend."

I take a moment to think. "It's very hard when you move around all the time and don't make many friends," I say. "I wish I'd gotten to know Zack better. That's all."

"Maybe you should tell that to his granddaughter."

"Yes, you're right." *Damn it.*

We return to the shop. "I'm sorry I acted so dumb," I say. It's all I can do to look at her. She doesn't act angry. She reaches out and hugs me, which startles me no end. *Jeez, two hugs in one day. A record. I'm not complaining.*

"It's all right," she says. "When bad things happen unexpectedly, we often say and do things we regret."

Well, that's interesting. But I'll bet I am her first albino freak. She doesn't understand that I always expect the worst. I'm programmed that way. Maybe my reasoning is faulty. Obviously, I didn't expect Zack to die. We all have to die. Tell me something I don't know!

"I'm really sorry to hear about Zack," I tell his granddaughter. "I only met him once, but he was very friendly and kind. I'll miss him."

The tears come. I can't stop them. They roll down my cheeks. Zack's granddaughter hugs me so hard, I can barely breathe.

"Excuse me," I manage to say.

"Yes?" she says.

"Do you have any tissues?"

"Sure." She runs to the back and returns with a box of Kleenex. I pull out a couple and blow my nose. My dark glasses are fogging up. I keep wiping tears, sniffling, and blowing my nose.

"My name is Sophia," she says. "And you two are . . ?"

"I'm Randy. And this is my friend, Portia."

"Portia. That's a pretty name. Portia was a wise woman in one of Shakespeare's plays."

Yeah, I know. "Thanks, Sophia," I say. "Your name is pretty, too."

"Um, Portia. Would you like to use my lens cleaner to wipe your glasses?"

"Thank you, Sophia. I'll ask one favor. Please don't freak out." Sophia smiles. She doesn't have a clue how I'm gonna rock her world.

I remove my sunglasses. Sophia's smile fades, but it doesn't disappear. She places a hand on my shoulder.

"You should have told me," she says.

"That she had pink eye?" Randy ventures.

We all start to laugh. "Wait! It gets better." I remove my ball cap, and my blue-streaked hair tumbles out.

CHAPTER 46

We say our goodbyes and run to catch the bus. We hardly talk, but it's okay. I like this friendly kind of quiet. We don't have to chatter about a lot of meaningless stuff to prove we're smart and like each other. On the ride home, I'm thinking, I need to tell Randy the complete truth, because that's what a real friend would do.

But first I need to warn Denise. Because I'd like to be her real friend, too.

I turn to Randy. We're sitting in our favorite spot in the back. He's next to his window, staring out, and I'm next to mine. The breeze ruffles my hair. "I just wanted to thank you," I say.

Randy shrugs. "Sure."

"Thanks for helping me get into the rehab place. I enjoyed meeting your dad, too. And thanks for being so nice when I found out about Zack."

Randy waves a hand. "Don't worry about it. You were nice enough to listen to my problems. What kind of a friend would I be if I didn't help you?"

Except I lied to you, Randy. I haven't told you everything. Like about Denise, your own girlfriend. She is your girlfriend, right?

At that moment, I realize Randy's never mentioned Denise. I wonder if he's told her he wants to break up. Could that be why Denise had me follow him? Might that explain why she thought he was cheating on her? Because she couldn't stand the idea that he'd simply lost interest in her. Plus, Denise has all these secret problems with her mother. And she feels like I'm her only real friend. And here I am— the most ridiculous spy who ever existed, who has developed a crush on her possible ex-boyfriend, who thinks I'm his friend for all the wrong reasons.

CHAPTER 47

I take my time unlocking my bike from the lamp post.

"Nice to see you, Portia," Randy says.

"Can I ask you something?" *Quick, before you leave.*

"Sure."

"Do you . . . have a girlfriend?"

Randy turns to face me. "Yeah, pretty much. You know Denise Laughton, right?"

Who doesn't? "Of course."

"Denise and I have been, like, going steady for a year or so. But things have not been good lately. Denise hasn't been happy. She won't tell me why. But I guess we're still going steady."

Oh, my God, Randy! If you only knew. If I only knew, for that matter. But you are so nice.

I remind myself that Randy and I are nothing more than friends.

"Portia? What's wrong?"

"Nothing." I turn from Randy and stow my bike lock inside its fitting. I'm getting out of here now.

"Portia?" Randy places his hand on my arm. I want to shake it off, but don't. "What's wrong?"

I'm frozen. I want to answer and I have no idea where to start.

"Are you pissed off at me?" he asks.

"No." *Not you, Randy. Anyone, but you.*

"Is it because . . . of Denise?"

That stops me cold. "I'm not angry. Just confused."

"Listen, Portia," Randy says. "Denise and I have our own friends. She has guy friends, and you and I can be friends, too. She knows that. Understand?"

I nod.

He smiles. "Take it easy, Portia," he says then turns to leave.

"Wait," I say, grabbing his arm. "I need to tell you something. First, I want to thank you for being such a great guy. Denise is lucky to be going steady with you." Randy starts to speak, but I raise my hand. "I also want to thank you for helping me out with Zack's granddaughter."

Now I have to tell him that I've been spying on him. And all I want to do is hug him.

CHAPTER 48

Before I can embarrass myself further, Randy says, "Don't worry about it."

Then, shock of shocks, he hugs me. I can't find the words.

"Friends, right?" he murmurs.

I grunt. My head is spinning. *Keep hugging me, Randy. My knees may buckle and I may fall down. It's okay.* "Here's the thing, Randy," I mumble into his ear. "I-I-I . . ."

"Well, look who's here," a female voice says.

I recognize it. Randy's arms release me and drop to his sides. I turn and see Mindy, flashing a sly look and waving her cell phone.

"Wait," I say. "This isn't what you think."

"Really?" She smirks.

I turn to Randy. Mouth agape, he looks at Mindy. "Mindy Robinson?" he says.

"Ye-e-e-s. That's me."

Then it hits me. Robinson. She's the daughter of Mr. Brown Suit Robinson at the rehab clinic.

"Hold it," I say. "Did you know . . ?"

"Well . . ."

"Known what?" Randy's eyes telegraph confusion.

"What I was about to . . . explain," I say, averting my gaze.

"All I know is what my father tells me, Mindy says. She turns to Randy. "I guess you didn't realize he was my father, right?" He keeps silent.

"So what's your point?" I'm not letting Mindy step all over Randy.

"My point," she says, hurling daggers at me, "is that you were doing Denise a big favor by spying on Randy. Turns out Randy wasn't cheating on her, but now he is cheating with you—with the girl she trusted to make sure he wasn't cheating with someone else."

"No!" I blurt. "We're just friends."

"Spying?" Randy pipes up.

"That's what I was about to explain." The words tumble out of my mouth. Randy's face is a blank slate. "You probably wouldn't believe a word I say, anyhow."

I take a deep breath, unable to say more. I wish I could disappear into the sidewalk.

"Hello. Remember me?" Mindy says. "You two can talk about whatever you want and believe what you like, but a picture is worth a thousand words. Don't you think, Portia?" Mindy leers at me and takes off.

CHAPTER 49

"Randy, I'm sorry." He looks at me and shakes his head.

"I was just going to tell you. Really. Denise thought you might be seeing another girl behind her back."

Randy's eyes widen. "Oh, my God. Well, that explains a lot." Randy works his jaw a bit but says nothing.

"I'm really sorry." I take deep breath. "Here's the whole truth. I hope you don't hate me for this. But I'll understand if you do."

I consider saying, *I'm so sorry. I'm a moron. I chose to help your girlfriend by spying on you because I was the only one she trusted, and she needs a friend. But then I got to know you and now I'm your friend, so I can't betray your secrets to her or anyone. ARGH!* I have a headache. I rub my temples with both hands.

"Portia? Are you all right?"

"I'm fine, Randy," I say to the sidewalk. "Just give me a moment."

I'm not fine. I'm the world's biggest liar. I feel like shit.

"I'll tell you everything. But first, I must call Denise and ask her to please not listen to Mindy or pay any attention to any dumb picture."

When Denise doesn't pick up, I leave a message. "Hi, it's Portia. We need to talk. I'll come over later." I must explain this in person. This is not voicemail material. Even I know that.

I tell Randy about Denise's note, meeting her in the gym, agreeing to follow him. I do not mention Kathleen or Denise's problems with her mother. That would make me a complete traitor. Eventually, I will tell her. All the secrets must come out.

"I'm sorry, Randy, and I'm so ashamed," I say. I fix my gaze on the sidewalk and wait for his verdict.

"That's the most unbelievable story I've ever heard."

I look up. Tears fill my eyes. I've had the wind knocked out of me, as if I'd fallen off my bicycle.

"It's been nice knowing you, Randy," I whisper and start to walk away.

"Hang on, Portia," Randy says. "Okay, I'm . . . shocked, of course. Angry. But I don't hate you." I sneak a sideways look at him. "You don't?"

"Not really. I'm angry at Denise. I wish she'd talked to me instead of using you to spy on me. Why doesn't she trust me?"

I hesitate before answering. "Well, as the world's worst spy, I'm in no position to tell you how to act, but maybe the lack of trust between you goes both ways."

He frowns and blinks twice. "And you've been caught in the middle."

"Nice work, Sherlock."

Randy's expression brightens. Denise has no idea how lucky she is.

Oh, my God! Denise.

"We need to go. Now. We need to find Denise and explain everything."

"Huh?"

"Mindy? The picture? Us? Hugging?" That is so not cool.

For the first time, I'm a passenger on my own bike. I manage to squeeze behind Randy. He takes the handlebars and off we go. I'm hanging on for dear life, the wind whipping through my freaky blue-streaked hair. For some reason, I don't give a rat's ass.

I'm on a mission. I want Denise to know that neither Randy nor I have betrayed her. And I truly want to be her friend. And Mindy isn't a real friend at all. Not really.

I must remind myself that Randy and I are just friends—no matter how cute he looks or how well he treats me. My arms are tight around his waist. "Let's all be friends," I say to myself. Because we can be friends, if we don't blow it.

As Randy pedals like mad, I'm thanking God that we live outside Gainesville, Florida, and not in New York City or Boston. I give thanks for living in a dinky town that has light traffic. We can ride our bikes like motocross riders and live to tell the tale.

When we reach Denise's street, Randy slows to take a hard right turn. The bike angles sharply. I lean into the turn. *Please, Randy, don't wipe out.*

When we make it, I exhale. Rolling down Denise's street toward her house, the air smells like fresh-mown grass. In big cities, the air smells of car exhaust and factory fumes. There aren't nearly as many trees or lawns. Or places to ride your bike. Just cars and buses and trucks everywhere.

Randy hits loose gravel and the front wheel wobbles. I'm hanging on for dear life. As I fear that Randy is about to completely lose control, we skid to a stop in front of Denise's house. "Well, here we are," Randy says.

"Phew!" *Thank, God.* Randy turns the wheel toward the curb. I get ready to dismount as Denise, Mindy, and Tara walk out the door.

CHAPTER 50

"Here they come," I warn Randy.

"Oh, no," he mutters, still fumbling with the bike. "I'll handle it. Don't worry."

"No," I say. "I got myself into this. I'll do the explaining. If you want to jump in, that's okay. But I need to do this." Randy grunts. I know he understands.

By the time he's secured the kickstand, Denise and her so-called friends are waiting nearby, arms folded.

I turn to Denise. "First of all, please just listen and don't jump to conclusions."

Mindy turns to Denise. "Didn't I tell you she'd say that? What would you expect her to say? Sneaking around with your boyfriend."

Denise's mouth puckers. She glances from Mindy to me. "What's going on, Portia? Why didn't you tell me?" Her voice is sharp. Something in her expressions tells me she's not in command.

I begin my defense argument. "Denise, I couldn't tell you what Randy was doing because I promised him I wouldn't.

Just like I promised you I wouldn't tell anyone about what I was doing for you. Does that make sense?"

The words hang there. I feel great relief. Finally, I've spoken the truth. I'm ready to face the consequences.

Mindy butts in. "Are you going to believe me, one of your oldest friends?" Or are you going to listen to excuses from someone you don't know all that well?"

I'd like to strangle Mindy. I resist. Tara grimaces, but gives me a thumbs up behind Mindy's back. I nod. I'm not going down without a fight.

"Gee, Mindy," I say. "If you're such a close friend of Denise's, why hasn't she shared *all* her problems with you?"

Denise perks up. Mindy freezes. "What?"

I ignore Mindy. *Ball's in your court, Denise. How do we play this?* Randy turns to Denise. "What problems? Why didn't you tell me?"

Nice going, Randy. Put on the pressure.

Denise says, "Hold on. I'll explain, Randy. First, I need to talk to Portia."

"I don't believe this," Mindy says. "You're going to let her fill your head with lies? After what she did?"

Denise holds her hand up in front of Mindy's face. "Stop talking. Now."

Mindy's mouth snaps shut. I steal a glance at Tara. She's smirking.

Denise pauses before turning to Mindy and Tara.

She speaks in a calm voice. "I'm going inside to talk to Portia. This won't take long. I'll be back in a minute."

Denise waves me toward the mansion and calls over her shoulder to the others. "I'll explain everything after we've had a chance to talk."

CHAPTER 51

As Denise and I cross the lawn, I can feel the stares of those left behind.

"This seems very surreal," I say.

"Don't worry," Denise says. "I wanted to talk to you anyhow."

I know. I remember. Then, Mindy and Tara showed up and we never got to talk. Plus, I shot my mouth off and ruined everything.

We enter the palace. She shuts the door firmly and heads toward the kitchen. I sneak a glance at the magic chandelier. This time it doesn't rope me in.

Denise opens the fridge and peers inside. "Shit. We're out of Coke. How about a Sprite?"

I'm too stunned to answer. Am I more stunned by hearing Denise say "shit" or that she's offering me a cold drink while her friends are standing around on the lawn. And here I thought I was the social moron.

"No thanks. I'm not thirsty." I feel bad for Denise's friends, even though one of them just tried to screw me over.

She pours herself a Sprite, not spilling a drop. She invites me to sit at the table. I wait to hear what she has to say.

"Portia?" Denise's voice pulls my attention back to her. "I . . . I don't know how to say this."

"What's wrong?" I try to keep my voice calm, but I want to grab her and shake her.

"Well, the thing is . . ." She pauses. "It's my mother."

This is torture. I want to shout, "WHAT about your mother?"

"What exactly is bothering you?" I finally ask. "And what does your mother have to do with it?"

I have no idea what I'm doing or if those are the right words, but I speak them anyway and hope for the best.

"My mother hates me," she says. I could almost cry.

"Why do you say that?"

"I'll never be as smart as she is."

"Denise," I say, fumbling for the right words. "I doubt your mom hates you."

"How would you know?"

Fair question. "Okay. Why would your mom hate you for not getting good grades?"

I feel awful saying it, but it's better than calling her dumb or stupid. Or slow. Those are horrible words I wouldn't use to describe anyone, not even my worst enemy. So I wait for Denise to respond. But she just stares back at me. "You don't understand," she says. "You couldn't."

She clutches her glass. I'm afraid it will break and cut her. "Never mind," Denise says. "Forget I mentioned it."

"Hold on," I say, raising my hand. "I need to tell you something."

"Is this about Mindy?"

My jaw drops. Denise may get bad grades, but she's no dummy. "Yes."

"I've known Mindy a long time. I figured she accused you of trying to steal Randy because she was jealous. You remember our talk here, right? About having real friends?"

"So, are you saying Mindy's not a real friend?" I ask.

Denise shakes her head. "Not exactly. Mindy and I have been friends for years, but she can be difficult. She's had . . . problems of her own. Like all the other kids, I think she is jealous of me. What she and others don't understand—just because I live in a big house and have lots of clothes doesn't mean my life is perfect. Tara glommed onto us last year. She and Mindy became friends." She pauses. "Sometimes I think Tara did it just to get to know *me*."

"When Mindy told me Randy was meeting someone secretly every week, I didn't know what to think or do. And I couldn't follow him, for obvious reasons."

"Did Mindy ever tell you how she knew about Randy?" I ask, thinking Mindy is getting off the hook too easily.

"She said she noticed Randy going to the bus stop one day. She saw him get on the bus. Then she noticed he did this every Tuesday."

I nod. "What made you think he was taking a bus to meet Kathleen?"

"Well, she's really cute and very smart. And Mindy thought she *may have* seen them together."

That answers my questions about Kathleen and why I was chosen for the ridiculous spy assignment. But why would Mindy say she saw Randy with Kathleen? And why wouldn't she take a picture to prove it? But I decide it doesn't matter.

"So, I guess you're curious about that picture of Randy and me."

Denise's chews her cheek. "Well . . . maybe."

"Please, let me explain."

Denise nods. "Okay."

"Denise, I'm a terrible spy. When I found out where Randy went on the bus, and why, I couldn't tell you everything. We ran into each other by accident. So I made up this terrible lie to cover my ass. And once he told me what was going on, I couldn't betray his confidence any more than I could betray yours. Can you see how hard that was for me?"

Denise looks up and nods. "Then why were you hugging him?"

"Once I got to know Randy, I couldn't believe how nice he was to me. I don't have many friends. You know that I've moved all over. I'm always the weirdo. Being the new kid on the block is hard enough. When you're also a pink-eyed, white-skinned creature, you'd rather be invisible than deal with other kids. But I was wrong. Randy proved that. I met a boy who thought I was cool."

Denise looks shocked. "Are you admitting you tried to steal him?" I hold my hand up. "I need to tell you more so you can understand the whole situation."

Then, I realize Randy needs to join us and share the missing piece about his father.

CHAPTER 52

I clear my throat. The confidence Randy shared was very private. So I'm not the one to tell you about that. He needs to do that. As for the hugging . . ." I feel a lump in my throat remembering Zach. "Randy hugged me because I'd just learned that someone I cared about had died."

I realize I'm grieving. This hits me so fast, tears well up in my eyes. I bite my lip. It seems ridiculous to cry over the death of someone I hardly knew. Yet, here I am stifling tears over a dead acquaintance.

Denise's look softens. "I'm really sorry. Was he a relative?"

"No. He was just, an old guy . . ." My throat constricts, so the last words come out with a squeak.

I feel so stupid. Like a baby. I don't want to cry and embarrass myself even more. This whole day has been one disaster after another.

"He must have been really nice," she says.

I nod, because I can't speak. "Let's ask Randy to come in," I whimper. I'm on the verge of tears and pinch my arm under the table. The pain distracts me and keeps me from breaking down further.

Denise gets up, leaving me a basket case, trying to hold it together.

"I'll be back in a minute," she says.

"Okay." I say the word, clear and strong, surprised at my ability to speak.

.I hear the front door open. "Hey, Randy? Can you come in for a minute?"

I hear Mindy and Tara's voices. They want to know what's going on.

"Okay, guys. Hold it." Denise shuts the door.

The front door opens again, then closes. Two sets of footsteps approach.

CHAPTER 53

Denise and Randy enter the kitchen. Denise fixes Randy a cold drink. Here we are, gathered around the kitchen table. I feel out of place. *What comes next?*

Denise speaks. "Let's talk. Portia, you start."

I freeze for a moment. Since I called this meeting, guess it's up to me to say why.

I swallow and clear my throat. "You two need to talk to each other, tell each other the truth." They look uneasy and fidgety. *And I wouldn't mind hearing all of it, either.*

"Randy, why don't you start?"

"Huh?" Randy looks panicked. "Why me?"

"Why not? C'mon, what's going on, Randy?"

He stirs his drink with his finger. "Well, I've been afraid to tell anyone this. I've been keeping a secret for years." He sounds weak and helpless. "Please, don't tell anyone else. If word gets out, I'll be in big trouble with my family."

Denise's look softens. She reaches out and touches Randy's arm. "I know how you feel."

"Really?" Randy's eyes wide.

"Just tell me, Randy. You can trust me to keep your secret. Honest." Denise sounds like she's pleading for her life. "I have secrets, too. I need to tell you both what they are—after you tell me what's going on with you and Portia."

"Randy and I are just friends," I tell Denise. "I got caught in the middle. Can you see that?" Denise looks uncomfortable.

I hold up my hand. "Don't worry, Denise. You'll get your turn."

Denise turns pale. I start to talk, but Denise steps on my words. "Wait. I'll tell you. But after Randy tells his side, okay?"

I take a deep breath and exhale slowly. *Finally, I'll find out what's going on.*

Randy sips his Sprite and turns to Denise. "I'm sorry I didn't tell you. I should have. I guess I was embarrassed. I've been visiting my real father."

"Your *real* father?" Denise peers at Randy. "I thought he was . . . dead or something."

"My mom acts like he's dead." His voice grows stronger. "But he's very much alive."

"Oh, my God."

Now I get it. Randy didn't tell me that his parents led him to believe that his real father was dead when he was actually very much alive. No wonder he's been hiding his visits.

"He's a recovering drug addict," Randy says. "I found out about him during an online search. My mom and step-dad would kill me if they knew I was seeing him."

"Now you know my secret, Denise. I told Portia after I got to know her, but I was afraid to tell you, because I thought you might not understand. Or you'd think less of me. When you started acting aloof, I thought you didn't like me anymore."

"I still like you, Randy. I was afraid I was losing you."

"Huh? You thought I was . . ." His voice trails off. He glances at me. "Oh."

"I didn't think I was losing you to Portia, of course." She chuckles then stops abruptly. *Of course, no boy would find me attractive.* Denise's eyes are sad. She must know she's hurt me. "I meant to say, I didn't know you had become friends with Portia."

"Who did you think I was seeing?"

"Kathleen Mahoney."

Randy's eyes get squinty. "Who?"

"C'mon, you must remember Kathleen. From summer camp?"

"Uh, there were lots of girls in camp. Which one was Kathleen?"

"My tennis partner. The cute redhead."

Randy rolls his eyes. "Oh, her. She was okay, but I didn't like her *that* much."

"So all this time, you've been seeing your dad."

"That's right. I haven't been sneaking around to see other girls." The corners of his mouth turn down.

"But you kept seeing Randy after you knew this?" Denise asks me.

"Randy and I had become friends." The words slip from my mouth. "I couldn't tell him everything. It wouldn't be right."

Denise hangs her head. "You're right." She takes a moment. Collecting her thoughts, I suppose.

"Okay," she says, "I need to tell you something. Randy, I hope it will make you feel better. And I hope you understand, Portia."

She stares at the window overlooking the beautiful garden. "My mother hates me, because I'm a poor student. I try to tell her it's hard for me, but she won't listen. She wants me to become successful like her, but I'm different. I'm not going to become a high-achieving businesswoman or a scientist or a brain surgeon. I want to be an artist. My mother says I'll never get anywhere in life as an artist. They don't think it's a real career. She's always putting me down."

"I wish I could go to art school instead of public school. My parents can afford it, but they won't pay for it. If I had better grades, I might qualify for a scholarship after high school. Then I could go to any school I wanted."

I think back to our conversation about the number of books I read. Now it makes sense.

"I can help," I say. "I'm helping Judy with math. You could study with us or you and I could meet."

"You would do that?" Denise's eyes light up. "You're a true friend. Judy is lucky to know you."

I nod. "So, have you been afraid to tell your other friends about your mom?"

"Exactly! I'm afraid to tell them, but not you. I feel like I can trust you completely, Portia."

For a moment, I feel ashamed. Why did I agree to help Denise? So I could go to her upcoming party.

"Am I any better than them?" The minute I say it, I want to take it back.

Denise nods like a ragdoll. "You're much better. My other friends wouldn't go out of *their* way to help me study. Not that they'd be such great teachers, anyhow. I've been feeling so bad for myself, I guess I've ignored you, Randy. I'm sorry."

"That's okay," Randy says. "But why did you think I was cheating?"

"I had my reasons. And you were acting squirrelly, keeping a secret from me. I could tell something was going on, but I was afraid you'd lie to me if I pressed. Just like I've been keeping my secrets from you. Understand?"

The way they look at each other, I know it's time for me to go.

I push my chair back and get up.

"I'll be outside with Tara and Mindy after you two have a chance to talk."

CHAPTER 54

I take my time crossing the lawn toward Mindy and Tara.

"What's going on?" Mindy demands. "What were you all doing in there?"

"That's none of your business." She raises a hand to her cheek, as if I've slapped her.

For a moment, Tara stares at me like I'm nuts. Then, her expression morphs into one of glee.

Mindy's face reddens. "I've known Denise much longer than you. Who are you to tell me what's my business and what isn't?"

"If Denise wanted you to know, she'd have invited you in." Mindy gawks at me. Wow, what a comeback.

She turns to Tara, who returns her gaze with innocent eyes.

Mindy turns for the house. "Fine. I'm going inside to find out what's up."

"You might want to think about that first."

Mindy pauses and gives me the once-over. "Why?" Her voice could freeze hot cocoa.

"They're discussing personal business."

Mindy gets in my face until our noses almost touch. "And I'm her best friend."

And this is the dumbest conversation ever. "Fine. Do what you want," I say. "But don't blame me, if she isn't happy to see you."

"You're jealous, because you wish Denise was your real friend."

"What would you know about that?" I say. "You have no idea what it means to be a real friend."

"Ha! Right." Mindy turns to Tara. "I'm going inside. Come on."

"No," Tara says, in a firm voice. "Leave them alone."

Mindy's face darkens and her eyes flash. "I don't believe this. What's *your* problem?"

"I'm tired of taking orders from you."

This whole situation is so crazy, I feel like I'm starring in *Bizarro World.*

Mindy stares Tara down. "So, you think you're in charge now?"

"No. Nobody's in charge. Not you or Denise. You're not the boss of me."

Tara says this without hesitation. Mindy says nothing, but her eyes reveal confusion.

Then Mindy snaps out of it. "Okay. So both of you are jealous. I'll leave you two alone, while I go check on my friend." She takes a few steps then pivots. "I hope you're happy, you freak." She turns on her heel and heads for the house.

"So long and good luck," I mutter before turning my attention to Tara. "What?"

"I've never argued with Mindy. Ever. This is the first time."

"And probably long overdue," I say. I've noticed how Tara kowtows to Mindy. "I'm sorry if I'm causing trouble, but I consider Denise a friend. And I don't think she and Randy want company at the moment."

"Don't you see what her problem is?" Tara says. "Mindy's so jealous of Denise and Randy, she'll do anything to break them up."

Oh, my God. Now it all makes sense.

"Did Mindy lie to Denise about seeing Randy with Kathleen?"

Tara shrugs. "Not lie exactly. Mindy hinted to Denise that Randy *might* be seeing Kathleen. We're the only ones who know about Denise's plan to spy on Randy. Ever wonder why? Because Mindy practically arranged it. I think she wanted to be the one to spy on Randy. Because I think she wanted to steal him. For years she's wanted to take Denise's place as most popular girl.

Now, I understand why Denise is so unhappy. This goes well beyond her home life. What kind of friend would do that to you? Being the most popular girl is much harder than I had imagined.

Mindy reaches the front door, and Denise and Randy come out. Denise doesn't waste a second. "I want you to leave now, Mindy." Her voice rings loud and clear. Side by side, Denise and Randy march toward us.

"Hey! Don't ignore me." Mindy's voice quivers. "Don't I get a chance to explain?"

Denise stops and addresses Mindy. "Haven't you done enough? You've lied to me for ages. You use me. What kind of friend does that?"

I'm replaying my decision to help Denise. Was I any better? Maybe Mindy has a reason for her behavior? So many questions. Maybe we're all assuming things about Mindy and then not checking on our assumptions. God knows, my assumptions about Denise were wrong.

CHAPTER 55

"Thanks, Portia," Denise says when she reaches me. "You're really a great friend."

"Uh, thanks."

"My birthday party is a week from Saturday. You're coming, right?"

"I . . . think I can." I'm feeling uneasy about this party now. Should I go? Do I deserve to go? And what about Mindy and Tara? I don't want to be at the same party as Mindy. I shoot Tara a look. She smiles back and nods. We're cool, I guess.

Mindy continues to glare. Then her expression collapses to one of pain.

"How can you do this to me?" she moans. "How could you?"

What is going on here? There's more to this than I imagined. Tara watches the scene unfold without weighing in.

Mindy's voice is husky. "I trusted you, Denise. I told you things I'd never tell anyone else."

"And I'm supposed to . . . what? Forget how you tried to make Portia look bad? Forget how you led me to believe

Randy was cheating on me?" Denise turns on Mindy. "You've been trying to take him away from me. And you've done your best to be me. Is that why you've stayed friends with me? Just to use me?"

"No." Mindy says without conviction.

"You've been jealous of me forever. And I've been putting up with it."

Mindy doesn't make eye contact. She seems to be counting the blades of grass.

"You see?" Denise says, turning to me. "This is my life. One thrill after another. Ha!"

"We all feel that way," I say. "Maybe Mindy should have a chance to explain herself."

Everyone looks at me like I've lost my mind. Even Mindy.

I'm not sure why I'm doing this, but it seems like the right thing. I know, deep down, that I helped Denise with her problem in order to help myself. Mindy has known Denise far longer than I have. She deserves a chance to tell her side of the story.

"Mindy, is there anything you'd like to say?"

Mindy looks pathetic. "I'm sorry. I fucked up. I've got problems, just like you. But I can't talk about them."

Tara looks dumbstruck.

A tear rolls down Mindy's cheek. I can't tell if she's a good actor or if she's in pain.

"Look, I'm sorry, okay?" Mindy's voice is hoarse. "Please forgive me."

Denise replies. "I'm not sure it's that simple. I know you've been through some terrible things. But you're asking a lot of me. I don't know if I can just forgive and forget."

"What things?" Tara pipes up.

"Mindy has told me about some . . . really bad stuff that's happened to her," Denise says. "That's all I'm at liberty to say."

Mindy wipes tears from her puffy eyes. "Okay, I've been a total asshole. Your life seems so perfect. Denise. And I don't blame you for being mad."

I think Mindy should talk to someone other than Denise. Maybe a mental health professional. Anyone with problems so severe that it drives them to hurt others in order to feel better about themselves needs help.

Everyone has problems. And everyone thinks their problems are the worst in the world.

For once, I know I'm not the only one who's completely clueless.

CHAPTER 56

So, it all boils down to this. Denise thinks her mother hates her, because she isn't cut out to be Superwoman or a Rhodes freaking scholar. Mindy has a horrible problem of her own that she confided to Denise. Meanwhile, Mindy wants to take Denise's place in the school pecking order, thinking it will solve her problems or at least make them less awful. As a result, Denise knows her so-called friends have agendas of their own and use their friendship to feel better about themselves. Denise has been afraid to reveal her secret problems, fearing that she'll lose everyone's respect. She relies on that respect, since she gets so little respect at home. She also feels like she can't trust anyone.

And that's why she turned to me, instead of Mindy. And that's why Mindy has always been suspicious of me. She's afraid I'm taking her place as Denise's best friend. Even though I'm the new kid and a colorless freak—a totally hopeless socially backward one.

It's so obvious now what I must do. What I have to do.

I don't know if I'm doing this right or not. But I'll do it and hope for the best.

"Far as I'm concerned, Mindy, I'm not holding what you said against you," I say. "So, don't worry about it. You and Denise should talk to each other. But I've explained the situation, and it's all cool. So, let's just forget about it, okay?"

Mindy's head snaps around. She looks at me with a surprised expression. "Really?" Denise looks at me and nods.

Tara gapes at me, wide-eyed.

Randy has been standing there, so quiet and almost bashful. It's like he wants out of this huddle of babbling girls. "Everyone deserves a second chance. Don't you think?"

Randy's eyebrows shoot up. My words got through to him.

"You're right," Denise says. She turns to Mindy, looking at her with an intense gaze. "You are my BFF. Let's talk about this later. Okay?"

Mindy nods. "Yeah, okay."

"I don't believe this!"

Everyone falls silent and turns to Tara, who looks thunderstruck.

"I'm going home," Tara announces. She turns and walks away. "I don't believe this shit," she says to no one.

"Wow, what's her problem?" Mindy asks.

"You'll never know until you ask her," I say.

Denise inhales deeply and exhales slowly. "This has been one really fucked-up day. I'm going inside to take a nap. Or a bubble bath."

She moves toward the front door, then stops and turns.

"You're still all invited to my party a week from Saturday. Are you coming?"

For once, I don't have a snappy response. "Of course, I'll be there. See you guys later." I glance at Randy. "Ready to go?"

"Well . . ." He looks at Denise.

Denise says, "If my parents were home, I'd offer you a ride, but they aren't. Sorry."

"That's okay. I'll talk to you later, Denise." He looks at Mindy. "See you later, too."

I have no idea if he's forgiven Mindy, and I don't really care. It's not my problem.

One thing has become quite clear. Randy and I really are just friends. And knowing that hurts more than I expected.

CHAPTER 57

After Randy bails out on me, I pedal straight home. I can't wait to get to my room and bury myself in a book. Real life gets way too exciting sometimes. Thank God for stories where people have even bigger problems than me.

Take that guy Holden Caulfield, for instance. He's so awesome, yet he has more problems than an old dog has fleas.

Or that Harry Potter kid. You'd think having magic powers would be great all the time. But I guess nothing is ever perfect.

So, I pull up in the driveway and lean my bike against the side of the house. I enter the front door and see my mom sitting in the living room. She's drinking a small glass of something that looks like flat cream soda. The TV is on, with the sound way down. My mom stares at the screen, like it's not actually there.

"Hi, Mom," I call, as I head upstairs.

"Portia?" Her voice stops me. She sounds helpless.

"Yeah, Mom."

"We need to talk."

Oh, no. This sounds serious. After today's fun, the last thing I need is a parental lecture.

"What's up, Mom? I've had a hard day, and I'd really like to go to my room and read for a while."

"Hard day, huh?" She sounds like she knows just what I mean. I hear the tinkle of ice, as she picks up her drink. "Maybe this is the best time to tell you then. Get all the hard stuff out of the way."

She pauses, then says, "Remember the first tooth you lost? We had to pull it, because it was so stubborn."

I nod, even though she can't see me. "Yeah." I'd been so scared it would hurt. But my mom tied a string around it and pulled it with no problem. "There," she'd said. "All done!" She'd hugged me and said, "See how brave you can be? Now . . . put the tooth under your pillow and the Tooth Fairy will leave you a gift tonight."

I'd put the tooth under my pillow that night, and in the morning, sure enough, there was a shiny quarter in its place. It was almost enough to make you believe in miracles, until I realized that the Tooth Fairy was my mom. Which was actually way more awesome.

So, I creep back down the stairs and peek into the living room. My Mom looks wiped out. Too tired to move.

"What's going on?" I walk toward the sofa and sit next to her.

Her expression remains somber, but lightens up a teeny bit. She reaches out to clasp my hands in hers.

"I have some . . . difficult news for you."

This is more than a bit weird. Usually, when my parents have bad news, they deliver it together. They take the tag-team approach to telling me things like, "We're moving again!" or, "Your report card says you don't talk to the other kids enough."

Rather than ask about my dad, I nod. "What now?"

My mother looks sad. I must have said the wrong thing.

"Your father and I have been going through a tough time," she says. "Your dad's job has taken a toll on all of us. I know it's been hard for you. Having to move all the time. I'm really sorry about that."

"It's not your fault," I say. "Dad has his work and we have to move a lot. That's the way it is, right?"

"Right." She says the word without conviction. "I'm not sure how to tell you this, so I'll just say it. You seem so strong, I keep forgetting that you're my child and I need to be more responsible for both of us."

"Your father and I are separating. I'm afraid this has been a long time coming. I want you to know that we haven't stopped loving each other. And both of us love you more than anything."

For a moment, I'm too stunned to speak. "Where's Dad? Has he left us or did you ask him to leave?"

My mom looks down at her lap. "I'm not explaining this well."

I think about what I just said and realize that it sounded like an accusation. I'm terrible at having these discussions. I feel so bad for a moment, I want to punch myself in the face for being stupid. Not really, but in my head.

Then, I realize my mom is doing the very same thing. And she's the adult and I'm just a kid. Why are we both doing this?

I decide it's time for me to let her know I'm not blaming her for anything, but I'd like to know the whole truth. I try to think of the right words before opening my mouth this time.

"Mom." I look directly at her, my voice pleading for her to meet my gaze. When she finally does, I say, "What I really meant to ask you is, if you guys still love each other, how come you're breaking up?"

She lets go of my hands, and reaches out to stroke my hair. "People can love each other and not be able to share their whole lives together. It isn't fair, but sometimes life isn't fair. We all have to make hard decisions about what we're willing to live with and what we can't.

"When it comes to your dad, work always comes first. That's the way it is, if he's going to . . . succeed." She pauses before finishing the sentence.

I want to tell her it doesn't matter. I've gotten used to moving and being the outcast freakazoid chick. In some ways, it's cool to be different. Who wants to be like everyone else, anyway? It hasn't helped Denise. If anything, it's made her life harder.

So, I say the first thing that comes to mind. "Don't worry, Mom. No matter what, we'll be fine. Moving around hasn't been all bad, even if it isn't the normal way to grow up."

In other words, I hope you're not breaking up because of me.

My mother senses the unspoken thought. "Our breakup isn't over you, believe me. It's just that your dad's career . . . always comes first. And what he does has affected my life, too. I have my own hopes and dreams. Your father's career has made it extremely difficult for me to choose what I want."

A part of me feels a rush of great relief. Then, I feel terrible again. I'm so glad this isn't all about me. But I feel bad that my mom has been suffering. And I've been so wrapped up in my own problems, I never noticed.

Is this what it's like to be an adult? And here I thought childhood was difficult.

"So . . . is Dad . . . just gone? Is he coming back to visit or how will this work, exactly? Will you guys share me? Trade me back and forth?"

I know of kids who've lived in two places, after their parents divorced. I figured that must be a little weird at first, but if you look at the bright side, this way you get the best of both worlds. You get to live in two different houses, instead of one. There's nothing like a change of scenery to make you realize how good you have it. Some people never go anywhere. In my case, I've been all over. What's the big deal about moving between houses? I can do it. I've done harder things and come out smiling, or at least not crying.

My mother takes a deep breath. "Here's where it gets complicated, honey. Your Dad will not be able to visit us. I'm hoping we'll see him once more, before he . . . takes this assignment."

"What? What kind of work is he doing that he can't even take the time to visit?"

"Honey, we've always told you your father was with the military. The truth is a bit more complicated. Your father works for the intelligence community. Do you know what that means?"

I nod, but say nothing. My heart is pounding and my head is spinning.

"We never told you before, for his protection, because in his line of work, it's essential to keep secrets, including what you do and who you do it for.

My mom grasps my hands again and looks into my eyes. "Your dad has been given a special assignment. The kind where no one can know where he is. Not even you and me. It's for his good and our own good. Do you understand?"

"Yeah." My voice breaks on the word, and I start to cry. My mom hugs me hard.

"There, there," she says. "It's going to be fine. Remember?"

I know, Mom. I have to get used to the idea that my dad is a spy. And I might never see him again.

CHAPTER 58

My mother tells me that Dad will be coming by a few more times before he starts the assignment. In fact, he's supposed to let her know very soon when it will start.

"I've been living on pins and needles, waiting to hear from him and trying to figure out what I should do," Mom murmurs into my hair. She squeezes me once more and pulls back to look at me. "I knew this would be hard, but I think I've made it harder by waiting to tell you. I'm sorry."

I don't know what to say. Should I comfort my own mother? Should I tell her I know what it's like to be a spy? Would that make things better or worse?

Finally, I say, "Mom, I'm old enough to handle this. It's not your fault things worked out this way. Life is just like that, right? Sometimes it isn't fair.

"This is going to sound . . . strange coming from a kid, but everywhere I've been, it's the same. I've been enough places to know that you can't always get what you want. People judge other people without knowing what's really going on with them. I always thought kids were the worst. I've been dying to grow up and get on with my life. But, now

I can see that being an adult means dealing with more of the same."

Here comes the hard part. I steel myself, because I don't want to keep crying forever.

"I'm sorry if I've been horrible lately. I'm just trying to *be* a kid and have fun. And I have to do it now, before it's too late. You know?"

My mom nods with sad eyes. "I know." She smiles. "My mother was right. You are quite a little lady."

"Thanks," I say, even though I still have no idea what she's talking about. I'm still trying to figure out how to be a happy kid.

φφφ

The next day, I go to school and try to act as normal as possible. During lunch, Judy and I sit together in our usual spot where we can view the room and be left alone.

"So, how are things with you?" Judy asks.

Got a couple of hours? I'm dying to say that, but there's so much I can't say.

I sigh. "Yesterday was . . . interesting. I found out Denise's secret problem and managed to get Denise and Randy to talk to each other. It turned out that Denise's best friend Mindy was using her. However, Mindy has a secret problem, too. So, instead of dealing with her problem, she tried to steal Denise's boyfriend. Except the plan backfired, because of me. So, Denise isn't as mad as she might have been, because having a secret problem makes you do crazy things. Like spying on your own boyfriend. So, we're all invited to Denise's party a week from Saturday. You can come with me, if you'd like. Um, Tara's pissed at everyone. And my parents are getting divorced. The end."

I'm staring at the table, and I heave another sigh before looking up at Judy. Her eyes are wide.

"Wow."

"I know."

"So what's Mindy's secret problem?"

"I don't know. It's a secret."

"So why is Tara pissed at everyone?"

"Because she's Denise's friend for the same reason everyone else is, and she feels like Mindy didn't get what she deserved, or something. I think. And people are mean and weird."

Judy shakes her head. "I'm really sorry to hear that. I'm also sorry your parents are getting divorced."

I realize my shoulders have hunched up while I was talking, so I relax them and breathe in and out.

"I was shocked," I admit.

"Are you okay?" Judy's coffee-brown eyes pierce me.

I wave the question away as if it were a gnat. "Yeah, I'm fine. They'd been acting funny, so I guess I should have expected this. I didn't know what was going on. And I can't talk about it."

Judy nods, but keeps giving me that quizzical gaze.

Finally, her expression clears and she says, "Well, I finally got a cell phone."

"Really? That's great."

"My mom was able to get a deal through her work. That's my big news."

"Awesome. So . . ." I manage to smile. "You want to go to a great big fancy party a week from Saturday? I'll be there."

Judy flashes her blinding smile. "Absolutely."

"Great. I'd hate to go without you."

"Thanks, Portia." Her look turns serious. "If you ever want to talk, anytime, you can call me now." We exchanged numbers.

φφφ

Getting through the rest of the day is much easier knowing that I have a real best friend in Judy, and I can talk to her anytime I like. She's trustworthy and kind, and I've proved myself to her, too. I think she understands the tough position I've been in with Denise and Randy, and Denise's so-called friends.

As I'm getting ready to call it a day, I think about this and realize that Mindy is Denise's friend, but made a terrible mistake, I guess. Who am I to judge her? So, if that's true, wouldn't that also be true for Tara? We don't know where Tara's coming from at all.

The more I think about the whole mess, the worse I start to feel. I feel a headache coming on as I close my locker and head down the hallway to the front door.

Before I am halfway there, Denise appears out of nowhere. Surprise!

"Hello!" she says, like she's singing it.

"Hi, Denise. So . . . we're not meeting in the gym, anymore, I guess?"

Denise pouts. "I deserve that. I'm sorry. I didn't mean to treat you like . . . I don't know."

"Like a freak?" I blurt. Then I feel horrible, because I have a headache and I know Denise has her own problems.

The corridor is nearly empty, except for a few kids who've hung back to watch us. Vultures. Denise leans toward me.

"You're not a freak," Denise murmurs. "You're much nicer than anyone else I know. And much smarter. I'd be lucky to have you as a real friend."

"Here's what I wanted to tell you. I've cancelled my big party. My mom will totally freak out, but I don't give a shit. It's my birthday, and I'll do what I want. I'm going to have a few friends over. I'd love it if you could be there. Call me later so we can talk."

For a moment, I'm speechless. "Well, sure. Can I bring my friend, Judy?"

"Of course, of course. Bring anyone you like." She glances at her watch. "Gotta boogie. My mom's picking me up. Talk to you soon. Or text me. Whatever!" She waves over her shoulder, as she scampers down the hall.

"Well, how about that?" I say to no one in particular. The kids who have been hanging around gape at me.

"Boo!" I yell. They run away.

Some things never change.

φφφ

By the time Friday rolls around, I'm anxious to get the week over with. I look forward to doing fun things with Denise and Judy. I hope they get along. I can't imagine why they wouldn't. Denise isn't a bad person. She just doesn't realize how lucky she has it compared to some people. Maybe meeting Judy would be a great thing for both of them. Or not. Only one way to find out.

I stow a few books in my backpack, close my locker, and leave school. Pedaling home on my bicycle, my blue-tinted hair, which is mercifully growing out, blows in the breeze. I'm looking forward to my next haircut. A style that's short and sophisticated, appropriate for a "little lady" and sufficient to eliminate all the blue streaks.

As I'm propping my bike on its kickstand, I hear his voice. "Hey, lady. Need any help with your luggage?"

I look up and see my Dad, smiling at me. He opens his arms.

I abandon the bike and run to him like a sprinter. When I reach him, my arms glom onto his shoulders. I hug him tightly, defying anyone to ever separate us.

"Dad, please don't go," I mumble into his neck.

"I'm sorry, kiddo." He keeps hugging me, and I can't stop the tears. He runs his hand through my hair. "I have to go. I don't have a choice. This assignment is important, and I must take it. They've insisted that I take it. They think I'm the only person who can handle it. And it's for national security reasons that I'm doing this. That's all I can say. I hope you understand. Do you?"

I bite my lip so hard I nearly break the skin. But I can't stop crying.

"Yeah, Dad, I do," I manage, between sobs.

CHAPTER 59

Three years later

So, I recently had my sweet sixteenth birthday. And my grandma made a great big deal about how these were the best years of my life or something. Sure, grannie, whatever.

I admit it feels odd, but also nice to have lived in the same place for three years. Most of the kids are still stupid, but I've figured out it doesn't matter. In fact, it's a benefit. I seem to have become a go-to problem solver.

I also have my own group I hang out with—the kids who have no group. You don't have to be one of the popular kids to do awesome things. And who would want to be one of them? It never helped Denise. Judy and I are still good friends, but Denise and Mindy were never quite the same after what happened. Tara moved the following year, and no one shed any tears. Go figure. I made good on my promise to help Denise with her studies, and she became a friend. But not like Judy. There are real friends and there are people you know. Judy's my real friend. Denise is a friend, maybe real or not. But I know her, and I'm willing to help her.

From what I heard, Mindy ended up seeing a shrink about her problems. I asked Denise what they were, but she still refused to tell me, even after her fallout with Mindy. Far as I'm concerned, Denise should get credit for that. She's Mindy's real friend, even if they aren't speaking to each other anymore.

I'm going to high school now, where Denise is just another pretty sophomore face. The competition is at a whole 'nother level. Fortunately, I was never in the race to begin with, so I'm happy to be a spectator to the ridiculousness of it. I still help Denise with her math problems. Her secrets are safe with me, as are Judy's. I'm good at keeping them. The perfect spy. How ironic is that? The freaky white chick who's invisible in plain sight.

My mother seems happy. She has a job as a real estate agent. And she's taking classes at the local university in order to get a B.A. She'd like to go on and get a Master of Library Science and then work as a business librarian. She's considered becoming what she calls an info-preneur, which I think is really cool. Now and then, we'll talk about Dad, but not too often. I think it's because we both miss him so much.

The day my father left, I had no idea it would be as if he'd disappear from the face of the earth. But that's what it's been like. In three years we haven't received a word from anyone about him. The first time my Mom called his office, she got the run-around from some guy who told her he had no idea who she was talking about. Then he hung up on her. When she called back she got disconnected.

For all I know, my father might be dead. For all I know, someone he worked for might have killed him. I've read some spy novels since he left. It's not all James Bond, fancy cars, gorgeous women, and champagne. It's dangerous work.

When you're caught in the middle, it's hard to know what to do. Whose side do you take? What's the right decision?

I feel my father's pain, having once been in a similar situation, although my life wasn't on the line.

So that's all I've got. If you're looking for some sort of moral, I couldn't tell you what it is. Don't follow strange boys riding on buses? Don't lie to your parents? Don't do stupid things just to be accepted? Feel free to take your pick.

I guess the point is that we all have to make choices. Up until three years ago, I never had to live with mine. I was always moving from one place to another, so I didn't have to choose to be anything anywhere. However, things changed once we settled here, and I had to decide who my real friends were.

I've heard we are the sum total of our choices. I've never been sure exactly what that meant until now. I'd like to think I add up to someone worth knowing.

Life is like a weird, crazy movie. It's like that novel, *The Sound and the Fury*. Have you ever read it? If not, I'll save you the trouble.

It starts out as gibberish—a tale told by a true idiot. Half the time, you have no idea what's going on. Slowly, the pieces come together. And just as it all starts to make some kind of sense, it ends—inconclusively. That's it.

You're welcome.

ACKNOWLEDGMENTS

I would like to thank my writer's group, including Ray Flynt, Lynda Hill, Mary Ellen Hughes, Sherriel Mattingly, Bonnie Settle, and Marcia Talley for all their support and helpful suggestions as I wrote this novel. I'd also like to thank the editor Beth Rubin and copyeditor Laurie Cullen, for whipping this story into its final form. I'm greatly indebted to all these people, as well as the graphic artist Kit Foster who designed the cover.

I can't begin to thank everyone who helped me reach the point where I felt ready to write this book. But I'd like most of all to thank my family and my husband, without whom none of this would be possible.

φφφ

ABOUT THE AUTHOR

Debbi Mack is the New York Times bestselling author of the Sam McRae mystery series. She's also had several short stories published in various anthologies and been nominated for a Derringer Award.

A former attorney, Debbi has also worked as a journalist, reference librarian, and freelance writer/researcher. Along with writing mysteries, Debbi is branching out into screenwriting and fiction writing in other genres, as well as contemplating other projects.

www.debbimack.com

CPSIA information can be obtained
at www.ICGtesting.com
Printed in the USA
FFOW02n1743110416
23146FF

9 780982 950883